INTERCHANGEABLE OMNIBUS

SADIE THATCHER

BEST OF FRIENDS

CHAPTER 1

"So this is your new job, Jacki?" Katie asked as her best friend showed her around the new salon. However, it was immediately obvious that it was more than just a salon. One wall featured four salon chairs, four stalls for hair styling and other beauty treatments. The other side of the shop looked as if it had come out of a tattoo and piercing parlor. But that was because it had. Jacki's new salon included tattoos and piercings too. And Jacki was certified to do it all. For the moment she was the only employee, but her boss was looking to eventually expand.

"That's right," Jacki answered. "And I want you to be my first customer."

Katie stood there, her hands fidgeting as she held them at waist level, just in front of her. She looked around the space, at the salon chairs and the mirrors, as well as at the wall with tattoo ideas and the jewelry cases, making it clear that this was a business that could do it all.

But then Katie's eyes fell on her friend. They had been best friends for years, but Jacki had been busy for the past few months, getting her certifications to begin this job, and in that time she had changed a lot. Her hair, once almost jet black and cropped short, was not long and blonde. Her body was improved as well. Katie never would have called her friend fat before, but she was definitely thinner now, able to wear a cropped top that showed off a hint of flat midriff and a small piece of jewelry in her navel.

"I guess I could use a trim," Katie said, referencing her chestnut hair that barely fell down to her shoulders. She had always preferred a short hair style, not wanting it to get in the way. Not that she ever did anything that made long hair a problem. She worked an office job, sitting in a cubicle all day.

"Great," Jacki exclaimed. "Now let's get you in the chair and I can get started. Don't worry, you never have to pay with me."

Katie climbed into the salon chair and got herself settled. Jacki busied herself with her supplies for a moment. Her mind was abuzz with possibilities. But when she turned around, she held a pink cape to cover her friend while she worked on her hair. Jacki snapped it open and then pulled it over Katie, being gentle but firm as she secured it around Katie's neck.

"You know," Jacki said with a devious smile. "I was thinking we should do more than give you a trim. Don't you think you'd look great as a blonde?"

Katie immediately scrunched up her face in disgust. "Why would you even suggest that? Can you really imagine me as a blonde?"

Jacki bit her lower lip as she decided how to best persuade her friend. There were a lot of arguments she could use, but in the end she decided that simple peer pressure was the best way to go about it.

"Oh, come on," Jacki said, almost begging with her tone. "I think you'd look so pretty as a blonde. Please, will you try it for me? It's not like you have to keep the color. Hair grows out. Or you can just come back and I can color it back to your natural color. No harm, no foul."

"Gee, I don't know," Katie said. She was already waffling, her determination against any drastic changes to her hair already beginning to fade.

"And just think, we could end up matching," Jacki pointed out. "Wouldn't that be kind of fun? I really think you should try it. It was a big step for me, going from black to blonde like this, but it was worth it. Believe me. I don't think I ever want to go back to black. I'm a blonde girl for life now."

Katie did not know what exactly did it for her, but something her friend said clicked for her. "Okay, I'll try it your way. Let's go blonde."

Jacki smiled brightly. "You won't regret this. I promise you. You're gonna love the way you look after this."

And so Jacki got to work. She had already been licensed to cut and color hair. Her time away getting certified had all been about learning the proper techniques for tattoos and piercings. But it was hair where Jacki got the most satisfaction. There was nothing better than helping a woman look her best. And even though she and Katie had been best friends for a long time, this was the first time that Katie had let Jacki touch her hair. And it was with that fact in mind that Jacki made sure she performed her absolute best work.

The coloring process was not short. The color needed to be stripped from her hair. And then new toner needed to be added, giving her a proper blonde look. There were smelly chemicals and foil wrapped hair involved, along with plenty of time, but Jacki was more than capable of giving Katie her full attention, making sure her friend came out looking perfect.

However, as Jacki worked, she began imagining other things she could do for her friend. In her time studying for tattoo and piercing work, she had learned about two different types of jewelry. There was the jewelry that most people purchased, the kind that simply looked good, and there was a new kind that tended to have a transformative effect on the wearer. That was how Jacki had lost weight. It was not that she had worked out, although she did have an improved fitness regimen now that her body was in better shape. It was that the jewelry she first wore had given her the kind of body that was enviable.

Katie had meant to only visit for a few minutes. She never meant to stay for what turned into three hours as her hair was dyed blonde. Not that she was in a hurry to get anywhere. Yes, she had work in the morning, but that was normal and her job did not require that much brain power. She had shown up without getting enough sleep the night before and done just fine.

"Wow," Katie said when she finally saw her finished hairstyle in the mirror. Jacki had kept her turned away from the mirror so she could not see herself in the various stages of coloring, knowing that her friend would probably freak out at some point along the way.

"Isn't it great?" Jacki said.

Katie found herself nodding her head in agreement. It was great. It was different, the color now more closely matching her skin tone instead of contrasting with it, but that was something she would just have to get used to. And if anything, her hair actually looked longer. Katie had no idea how Jacki had done that, but her usual shoulder length hair seemed to be about an inch longer than she remembered it. Not that Katie thought about it all that closely. The fact it looked good was all that mattered.

"Okay, since you like your hair so much, can I make another suggestion?"

"Sure," Katie said, still enamored with her reflection and only half paying attention to Jacki's words.

"I think you should get your belly-button pierced. It'll look good and it will literally change your life for the better."

Katie tore her gaze away from the mirror and looked into Jacki's eyes, trying to get a read on her. Was she really suggesting that or was she just joking around? Jacki was usually pretty serious about these sorts of things, but she still had her moments where she liked to joke and kid. However, as soon as she saw the hopeful look in Jacki's eyes, she knew her friend was not joking. She was completely serious.

"I don't think I'm a good candidate for that kind of piercing," Katie argued. Even though she was still covered by the salon cape, she knew what her body looked like beneath it. Her office job had her sitting for long hours and she rarely exercised. Katie was a healthy eater, believing good nutrition was important, but even the healthiest of meals could not prevent the effects of her sedentary lifestyle.

"Nonsense," Jacki countered. "You have to trust me. You're gonna look great after this. I was right about your hair, wasn't I?"

Again, Katie found herself waffling. She wanted to say no. She really did not think a belly-button piercing would look good on her. Plus, she thought they had gone out of style. And yet, she felt the pressure Jacki put on her. She did not want to upset her friend.

However, a piercing was different from a new hair color. Hair could be redone. A piercing was kind of permanent. She knew she could always take out the piercing and the hole would eventually close up, but there would always be a mark from it, a tiny scar from where the hole had been made.

"Yes, you were right about my hair—"

"So you'll let me pierce your belly-button?" Jacki asked excitedly. She acted as if being right about one thing made her right about everything else.

Katie did not answer right away. She wanted to say no, but the pressure to agree with her friend kept building higher and higher. It should have been easy to stand her ground, but something about the moment felt different. Katie caught sight of her reflection again and found herself admiring her hair. Jacki had been right about that. She looked fantastic as a blonde. And if Jacki's suggestions played out similarly, Katie felt like she needed to give it a try.

"Yes, I'll do it," Katie finally relented.

In all, Katie spent four hours at Jacki's new salon. She had meant to just stop in for ten minutes. But as Katie left that evening, already yawning and wanting to go to bed, she had to admit she was happy that her visit had gone so well. She was still not sold on the navel piercing, but Jacki had made her promise to give it a couple days at least. If she was not happy with it by then, she could of course take it out.

However, there was surprisingly little pain coming from her midriff. The piercing gun had not even really hurt. And as Katie thought about her visit with Jacki, she was faced with the realization that her friend had not even given her aftercare instructions. But that was something she could do in the morning. For now, she just wanted to crawl into bed and fall asleep.

And when Katie woke up the next morning, she once again felt no pain from her new piercing. But that was not at the forefront of her mind. Something else was drastically wrong. Or maybe it was right. All Katie knew was she needed to call her friend.

"Jacki, what the hell happened to me?" Katie practically screamed into her phone as she paced around her bedroom. She had woken up to find years of weight gain around her middle and simply melted off her body. It was like it was never there. For the first time in many years, Katie was thin.

"Is something wrong, babe?" Jacki asked in return, playing it cool.

Katie was so caught up in what had happened to her, she did

not notice how her friend had called her "babe". Jacki had never spoken to her that way before, using such language to describe her. Katie had never been a babe, although now that she had dropped all of her excess weight and actually looked somewhat fit beneath her now oversized pajamas, she could almost be considered a hot babe. Almost.

"What happened to all my weight?" Katie asked, her voice calmer now than when she first made the phone call. As much as waking up like this was a surprise, she had to admit she liked the results. She felt attractive for the first time in a long time.

"It was the piercing," Jacki said excitedly. "That's how I lost my weight too. Isn't it great? You wear one pretty piece of jewelry and your whole life is improved."

Still pacing around the room, holding up her pajama pants with her free hand as she pressed the phone to her ear, Katie was really beginning to feel at peace with her situation. It would have taken her months, if not years, to drop all that weight, taking the long path of eating healthy and exercising religiously. Katie was not sure if her new figure could be maintained just by wearing her new jewelry, but she had already decided that it would be staying.

"I mean, yeah, it is pretty great," Katie finally admitted out loud. "But you could have warned me. With my blonde hair, I bet no one at work will even recognize me. And I just realized I don't have any clothes that fit me anymore. You should have warned me."

Katie could hear her friend's apathy through the phone. She could just tell that Jacki did not really care about that aspect of what had happened between them the night before and the consequences that Katie was now living with. Then again, they were welcome consequences. Sure, they were annoying as hell, considering she needed to be at work soon and she had nothing to wear, but going shopping when she was confident that clothes would actually fit her now was no longer the chore it once was.

"See?" Jacki said. "Nothing to worry about. Now I've got to go. Something has popped up that I need to take care of."

Even though Katie knew her friend well, she had no idea that Jacki had a man in her bed and that as he roused himself from sleep, his cock had started to rise. She had no idea what she had interrupted when she called.

However, instead of going straight to her closet to try and find something she could wear, Katie found herself stripping off her pajamas and standing in front of the mirror, enjoying her new look for the first time. She had no idea how she was going to explain away these changes when confronted by her work colleagues and her boss.

"I'm not sure I would have chosen pink," Katie commented as she looked at her new piercing. She was surprised to see that it looked relatively healed. She would have expected some redness or swelling, but there was nothing. There was no pain. It was like magic. Then again, losing all those pounds from her body overnight was magic too, so Katie was in no place to argue. "I guess it looks good though."

And it did. Katie had never had a body where a belly-button piercing would have looked good. Now she did. Her felt and toned midriff was ideal for showing off a little bling. And pink was not bad. It was just more feminine than Katie was used to highlighting. Not that anyone from work would get to see her new addition. Office dress codes would have precluded such a possibility.

By the time Katie did finally get herself into work, she wore the smallest dress she owned. It was still baggy, but it maintained some degree of office appropriateness. It was definitely long enough, but it was far too loose in the chest. Katie was forced to wear a sweater that had shrunk in the wash on top, just to keep herself from leaving too much on display.

No one noticed any changes in Katie that day at work. However, she did not leave her cubicle the entire time she was in the office. She hurried through her work, racing to get done so that she could leave early and go shopping. For once she was actually looking forward to buying new clothes. She no longer needed to worry about looking frumpy. She could wear the latest fashions. She just had to learn what those were first.

CHAPTER 2

It took a week for Katie's colleagues to notice the changes in her appearance at work. By then she had stopped hunkering down in her cubicle everyday. She walked around, wearing fitted blouses that hugged her improved body and either knee-length skirts or fitted slacks, both of which did a good job of highlighting her butt.

Jacki had kept tabs on her friend, although only through text messages. They had not spoken since that early morning phone call. There were supportive messages and requests for pictures of Katie wearing her new outfits. It had taken until the weekend, but Katie had gone shopping for a second time, focusing on clothing she would wear outside of work. Jacki was extra pushy about getting shots of those. Katie even bought a few midriff baring tops. If she had a belly-button piercing, she might as well show it off. She had the midriff for it.

The biggest change that Katie experienced after her massive body change was how people treated her, especially men. She had always gone through life as a wallflower, as someone who blended into the background while the important or attractive people ignored her. She was not getting ignored anymore.

Between her slim body and blonde hair, she was attracting a lot of attention.

At first that attention bothered her. Katie was not used to it and she would turn red whenever someone paid attention to her. She was even getting asked questions in meetings. Her name had never once been called before.

But after a while, a couple weeks, that attention was starting to go to Katie's head. She not only came to accept it, but to expect it. And when she did not get it, when one of her colleagues ignored her for the new blonde receptionist with a large chest, she seethed inside. She wanted people to keep paying attention to her. She wanted to grab the guy looking at the new receptionist by the collar and drag him away. And for some reason that turned her on more than she could imagine.

For the first time in her life, Katie found herself wanting to be more sexual. That was why the night before she had made an appointment to return to Jacki's salon to have her hair done again, her roots needing to be touched up, she found herself out at a bar, wearing one of her midriff baring tops and a pair of tight pants that really emphasized her ass. She was not big back there, but she still looked good in the right pair of tight pants.

"You're cute," the man said. Katie did not know his name, but he had just walked up to her as she stood at the bar, waiting for a drink to be made.

It was by no means the best pickup line in the world, but Katie looked up at the tall man who said those words and swooned a little. He did not need to make a bold move when he looked that handsome. He was the epitome of tall, dark, and handsome, complete with a strong jaw.

When Katie's drink arrived, he slapped down a bill and told the bartender to keep the change. Katie giggled at the treatment, loving it. She had never had someone buy her a drink before. Her few dates she had gone on always seemed to have her paying for her part of the occasion. And all it took was a simple belly-button piercing to get her to be noticed by a hot guy.

It was only an hour later that she was back at her apartment, large trash bags of her old clothes still sitting in a corner, waiting to be donated to charity, but with Katie's hands all over her gentleman caller as she pulled him into her bedroom. His hands lifted her top further up her torso, until her bra was exposed. As she pulled him down onto the bed with her, her hands went to his belt, working to free him so that he could fuck her.

"Yes," Katie moaned the moment his cock pushed into her pussy. She could not remember the last time she had sex, but she was certain it had no felt this good. Her eyes rolled up into the back of her head as he thrust in and out of her. He had shared his name. It was Alan, but names meant nothing as her body pulsed with pleasure. Her whole body had entered a euphoric state of orgasmic pleasure. She just needed to cum and everything would be right with the world.

Time lost all meaning as Katie was stuck on the precipice. Each thrust had her calling out in need, begging to cum, but Alan did not change his pace. He took his time, playing Katie's body like a musical instrument. He was not just handsome, but incredibly capable when it came to sex as well. He knew how to use his cock.

"Fuck yes," Katie finally cried out when she came, her body convulsing as a wave of pleasure washed through her body. Alan came too, his cock surging with hot white seed, but his orgasm paled in comparison to what happened to Katie. Every nerve in her body resonated with the pleasure, giving her a whole body orgasm that she did not even know was possible before. It was a life changing experience that put a smile on Katie's face.

And that smile was still there when Katie arrived at the salon to meet Jacki. This was an after-hours appointment. It was free, so it made no sense for Katie to take up valuable business time.

Besides, Katie had work. And even though she nearly got chewed out for a small mistake on a report she had created, she was still smiling, her body practically glowing after her extraordinary orgasm the night before.

"Someone got laid last night," Jacki called out as soon as she saw Katie enter the salon.

"What?" Katie asked, shock spread across her face. "How did you—"

"You've got the look," Jacki explained. "I have it most days. Now get over here so I can get a look at you and then we can get started."

Katie had little time to contemplate what her friend meant by her having a freshly fucked look on most days. Instead, she found herself quickly pushed down into the salon chair with a pink cape covering her body. Katie had originally planned to come to the salon straight from work, but she realized she had some extra time, so she stopped off back at her apartment and changed clothes, choosing a tight top that showed off her belly-button and a pair of shorts that were almost short enough that her butt could fall out. Almost.

"Your hair is really coming along great," Jacki commented as she began her work. It was a lot easier just touching up the roots than it was to dye everything.

This time Jacki did not try to hide Katie's appearance from her. She faced the mirror, but instead of looking at herself as Jacki performed her work, Katie instead found herself looking at her friend's lips.

"Whoa, did you get stung by a bee?"

"My lips?" Jacki automatically said. "Do you like them? I love them. I've been putting them to a lot of use lately."

Katie did not know what her friend meant, but she simply shrugged her shoulders and went along with Jacki's explanation. It made little sense to her that Jacki's lips had been put to a lot of use. She never imagined that Jacki had been sucking lots of cocks.

"They're different, but they look good," Katie finally decided, giving her friend her approval.

"Ooh, I know just what you need when I'm done with your hair," Jacki said, practically jumping up and down on the balls of her feet with excitement. Except she did not say anything more. She shut her plump lips and smiled as she continued working on Katie's hair.

It was only afterward, once Katie's hair was completely blonde again, that Jacki decided to fill in her friend. "I think it would be really hot if you got your tongue pierced."

Katie raised her eyebrows at that. It was one thing to pierce her belly-button. That was normal. Many women had that done. But her tongue seemed to be a stretch too far.

"I won't be able to speak with something like that in my mouth," Katie objected.

"Sure you will. Do I sound any different?" It was only then that Jacki opened her mouth enough for the pink stud to appear between her parted lips that Katie realized that her friend really did have a tongue stud. And even with her now inflated lips and the stud in her mouth, Jacki sounded completely normal. There were no impediments in her speech at all.

"No, I guess not. But what will people think about me at work?" Katie objected. However, her feelings were already starting to turn toward letting Jacki pierce her tongue. She was being a pushover and she knew it, but she had a hard time saying no to her friend.

"How much do you really speak at work?" Jacki countered.

Katie immediately thought back to the past several weeks, ever since her coworkers started noticing her weight loss and improved figure. They had been asking her more questions, but that did not mean they were looking at her mouth when she spoke. She had a feeling that many of them, especially the men, were not looking at her face, but at the rest of her body. She was not well-endowed, but her slim figure in her fitted blouses were definitely eye-catching.

"Okay, fine," Katie relented. "But if I don't like it, I'm taking it out."

"Of course. But you've got nothing to worry about."

Unlike last time, Katie did not need to simply sit there with her top pulled up around her middle. This time she needed to stick her tongue out. Worse, Jacki grabbed it with a pair of forceps and pulled her tongue out even farther, making sure she got the perfect placement for the piercing gun.

Katie grimaced, expecting pain, but the piercing gun went in painlessly. And before she knew it, her tongue was back in her mouth with a small piece of metal sticking through it. It was done.

"Don't try to speak right now," Jacki said as Katie started to open her mouth. "I know I said it wouldn't be a problem, and it won't, but you've got to wait until tomorrow before you start into any oratory. Tonight, just keep your mouth shut. Except for looking at that beautiful pink stud in your mouth. I just know you're going to love it."

Katie made her way home, her body responding similarly to how it did the last time she got a piercing. She was tired. She wanted to go to sleep. And that was just what she did.

CHAPTER 3

"Fuck, you're a great cocksucker," groaned Katie's boss. She had come in to deliver a report to him, but she had found herself on her knees in front of him, his cock in her mouth, before she even realized what was happening. He came quickly, coating her tonsils with his cum. "I love our mornings together like this."

Katie was not sure how her life had changed so dramatically in the last several weeks. The day after she got her tongue pierced, she woke up with thick, plump lips, just like Jacki had. She should have expected it. She should have connected the dots. But it was too late now. Not that Katie was unhappy with the fact she had sucked more cocks in the last several weeks than she had ever seen before all of this started. There was something about wrapping her lips around a cock that just felt so good, so right.

It was also unclear when she had started mixing business with pleasure. Every time a cock ended up in her mouth, everything went a little hazy. She got so turned on by it all that her memories became foggy. And almost every time, she would need to go off to the restroom and get herself off before she could go back to work.

And it was not just Katie's boss that had taken advantage of her new proclivities. She had sucked off the entire sales team when they made their monthly quota. She had even given the mail clerk a blowjob when he delivered a package to her cubicle. She had licked her lips when she saw him and then dragged him over to the printer room where she dropped to her knees and gave him the best blowjob he had ever had, or would ever have again.

Katie would have been mad, but it all felt so good. She was constantly licking her lips. That or she was checking her makeup, making sure her lipstick looked perfect. She had twice found her own lipstick stains on a man's cock, them trying to come back for a second round. But as much time as Katie was spending with a cock in her mouth, she was still getting plenty of work done. And it was not like her pussy was getting neglected.

Katie had started going out three to four nights per week, always picking up a guy who she brought back to her apartment and both sucked him off and fucked him until she came. There had been a few times she was late getting into the office, because he was still in her apartment the next morning and she had been unable to stop herself from a second round herself. Those were days when she made sure her boss got at least two blowjobs, making up for her being late.

Miraculously, Katie was still getting all of her work done. Some of it she successfully pushed off onto others, never explicating trading blowjobs for them doing her work for her, but some of them might have taken it that way. They were always happy to oblige her. And she did not do that for everything. Her latest report to her boss was all her own work. It might have taken an extra day, but it got done within a reasonable amount of time.

"You're doing great work these last couple weeks," her boss said. "I don't know what this company would do without you."

Katie smiled as she pushed a small dollop of cum that had escaped her lips. She was good at swallowing everything down, but every once in a while a little escaped the corner of her mouth. Her lips did not seal as well as they used to, their increased size often leaving her with a small keyhole pout.

"I always try to serve, sir," Katie answered before she rushed off to the restroom to get herself off. She would rather get a cock in her, but somehow she felt that would be a step too far while at work. It was one thing to hand out blowjobs like they were candy, but it was another to take up even more time by getting railed by her coworkers.

When the workday ended, Katie rushed home so she could change out of her stuffy work clothes. Sometimes on the drive home, she would take off her blouse, driving home wearing just her bra on top. Somehow the less clothing she wore, the better she felt. It seemed more natural that way. Her skin needed to breathe.

But the reason for her rushing was not because she just wanted to get home and away from the office environment, which she definitely did, but because she had an evening appointment with Jacki. Or actually, as Katie had been told now several times over the past week, it was Jaci now. Her friend had not given a reason for the name change, but Katie had no problem with it. It removed a letter from her name and changed the pronunciation, but she would call her friend whatever Jaci wanted to be called.

"Hey, girlfriend," Jaci said with a big smile as Katie walked into the salon. She had swapped out her office blouse for a cropped halter top and wore a short skirt with slingback heels. Katie thought she might go out after getting her hair touched up, so she wanted to look good. That meant plenty of makeup too, especially the wet look pink lipstick that she liked to wear when she was looking to suck a cock.

However, Katie's eyes nearly bugged out of her head when she saw Jaci. Her best friend still sported the blonde hair, the thin figure, and the plump lips, but she now had large tits. They were gigantic compared to Katie's tiny boobs. Sometimes Katie wondered why she even bothered with a bra, until she decided to wear the bra as a top on her way home from work, that is. But Jaci was definitely sporting a new look. Her low-cut top showed off not just a valley of cleavage, but the rounded tops of her breasts made them look fake.

"You like my new girls?" Jaci asked as she shimmied her shoulders back and forth to make her tits jiggle. Although their movement was limited. These were not the super soft natural breasts that some women had that jiggled and bounced all the time. They were firm and round, very round.

"They're…" Katie started to say, but then she faltered, not knowing exactly what she thought of them.

"They're awesome," Jaci said, filling in Katie's statement with her own opinion of her new additions. "And they feel so good too."

Katie shivered, unable to look away from Jaci's clear delight in her expanded bust.

"When did you get them done?" Katie asked. "It couldn't have been that long ago. We saw each other four weeks ago."

Jaci did not answer. Instead, she beckoned Katie to sit in the salon chair so her roots could once again be touched up. Even if Katie and Jaci had not said anything about trimming her hair, that was not on the menu and it had not been since all of this started. Hair was not supposed to grow as fast as Katie's had, but where it had once been shoulder length, it now ran halfway down her back. Katie certainly was not complaining. She was not sure when she would start getting it cut again, but even though the longer hair required more work, she loved how it looked too much to trim it back.

Katie let herself sink into the chair and allowed Jaci to get to work. Her friend was efficient, coloring her roots until they were a perfect match with the rest of her hair. With the lips and the narrow waist, Katie was starting to think she looked like a Barbie doll. Actually, Jaci looked even more like Barbie, with her big tits. Katie actually found herself jealous.

"Time for another piercing," Jaci announced once Katie's hair was done.

"What this time?"

"Nipples. That's what you need. Trust me."

This time Katie was wise to the situation. Every change that Jaci had undergone, Katie had undergone as well. And each one was precipitated by a new piercing. The belly-button piercing had given her a tight and toned body. The tongue piercing had given her bee-stung lips and a penchant for sucking cock. And if there was one thing that Katie was certain of, the nipple piercings would give her tits like Jaci.

"But what if I don't want big tits like yours?" Katie asked, although her actions belied her words. She had already reached up and had begun untying the straps behind her neck so that her breasts would be freed for Jaci to do her work.

"You know you want them," Jaci answered. Katie simply nodded. Once her chest was bare, she sat back and let Jaci get to work. Her friend was an expert at piercings. And nothing had gone wrong so far. Yes, she had some unexpected outcomes, but even now, Katie could not find fault in any of them. Her behaviors had changed, as had her style, but Katie had never been happier.

And before Katie knew it, she had pink barbells sticking through her nipples. The pain was minimal and even sitting there for a few more minutes, waiting for the slight throbbing to disappear, Katie imagined what it would be like to wake up in the morning with a set of tits like Jaci. She could not wait.

As it turned out, there was no going out after her appointment with Jaci. Katie should have anticipated something like that, but she did not regret her decision to get dolled up for the evening. She actually had started to prefer looking this way. Yes, she had the look of a blonde bimbo, but Katie was still a smart and capable woman. She just had an overactive libido that led her to fuck and suck more often than was strictly necessary. She went straight home and turned in for the night, a smile on her lips and she dreamed what life would be like with bigger tits.

It was a weekend spent shopping. Some of Katie's clothes still fit her expanded assets, but her big, round tits definitely stretched some of her tops beyond what they were designed for. Not that Katie minded. She loved shopping now. And she even managed to snag an employee discount a couple times by flashing her new tits or sucking a cock. She was having fun and being practical.

But everything came to a head Monday morning. She arrived at work a few minutes late. It was not a lot, but everyone else was already present. And the way Katie's blouse was left unbuttoned almost to the point that her bra wanted to peek out, it was clear that not only was everyone going to look at Katie as she walked into the office, but she wanted them to look. She was showing off.

Katie did not even stop at her cubicle. She went straight to her boss' office. As soon as the door was closed behind her, she started to strip off her blouse. Her bra was next.

"Sir, I want you to break in my new titties."

Her boss was speechless, but he pushed his chair away from his desk and gave her room to maneuver. She drooled into her cleavage, getting her tits wet. Then she wrapped her lips around his hard cock, wetting him for the main event.

Katie had been dreaming about this moment all weekend. Every step was planned. She was the hottest woman in the office and she wanted to not only make every man drool over her hot body, but she wanted to secure her job by making sure her boss had every reason to keep her around. Getting work done was no longer a worry for her. But if she kept making sure her boss got full access to her smoking hot body, she was certain her job would remain safe and secure for as long as she wanted.

"Oh, those are nice," her boss groaned as she slid up and down on his cock, pushing her big tits around his shaft. And every time the head peeked out from between her tits, she reached out with her tongue and gave it a little lick. Every little bit counted.

"Clancy," came a shrill shout from the door.

Katie's boss looked up and froze, but she kept working his cock, not bothering to look at who was at the door. Although she realized that she had not locked his office door behind her. Had that been a mistake? She usually did that, but the idea of her getting caught with her boss was such a turn on.

"Katie, you're fired."

The words were so final that it took her a moment for them to sink in. The woman who had caught them turned out to be her boss' wife. He was married. Katie had not cared. Rings meant nothing to a slut like her. What mattered was whether he had a cock or not. She did not even look at his hands before she had turned into a hottie.

But even Katie had to admit that her full-proof plan to never get fired had a fatal flaw. She never expected to have her boss' wife catch her in the act. He'd probably be forced to get a divorce too, which meant she could have free access to his cock again. However, that was assuming he kept his job. If his wife wanted to push her case, his ass was on the chopping block as well.

And so Katie was fired. Her blouse stuck to her wet breasts, but she did not care. This time she did stop at her cubicle, making sure to collect any personal belongings that she had stored there, before she made her way back out to her car. She was gone an hour after she had first arrived. But what was she going to do now?

CHAPTER 4

Katie went to the only place she knew to go. She showed up at Jaci's salon. It was quiet, still being early on a Monday morning.

"Hey, babygirl," Jaci called out upon seeing her friend. "You're looking, like, so hot right now. But, like, why aren't you at work and stuff?"

If Katie were not so distraught about losing her job, she would have noticed the peculiar way her friend was speaking. Jaci had over the weekend adopted speaking like a bimbo to go along with looking like one. Little did Katie realize that this was the new and permanent Jaci. She really was a bimbo now, through and through.

"I got fired for giving my boss a tittiefuck," Katie complained. "His wife walked in on us."

"Oh, come here, babe," Jaci said, mincing over to her friend so that she could wrap Katie up in a big hug.

Katie let herself relax into Jaci's embrace, feeling her warmth and caring nature. Jaci really was her best friend. She always had been, but now it felt more real than ever. They were both on similar journeys. They even had started to look so similar.

Long blonde hair, tight bodies, plump lips, and big tits. They were almost mirror images of each other. Except there was something extra in Katie's eyes. There was an intelligence there that Jaci no longer had.

Eventually Katie and Jaci's hug had to end. A customer came in for a hair appointment. Katie sat back and watched as Jaci worked. More and more it looked like Jaci barely had a thought flitting around through her head. But the more Katie watched her friend, the more she realized how happy Jaci was. It seemed as if every part of her life was perfect. She got to help make other people prettier, by doing their hair or giving them tattoos or piercings, although Katie guessed the customers were not treated to the same piercings that Jaci or Katie got.

When the customer finally left, Jaci returned to Katie, sitting beside her and relaxing.

"I know what you should do," Jaci suddenly exclaimed. That was followed by a giggle. She had been doing that all morning, but it fit so easily with her sunny disposition. "You should, like, start working here with me."

Katie looked concerned. That was not how she understood these things to work. Katie would need to go to beauty school. She did not have the money for that. She did not even know how she was going to pay off her credit card bill next month when all the clothes she bought over the weekend came due.

"Don't look like that," Jaci said. "It'll be fine. Johnny, the owner, has been looking for a new girl to join me. He's even willing to, like, pay for training and stuff. He's super nice and a total hottie." Jaci giggled as she thought about her boss. It was clear that Katie was not the only one of them who had been getting busy with their bosses. Only Jaci had far more protection it seemed. Katie was jealous of her friend.

"I guess I could do that," Katie said, still considering her friend's offer. She needed a job. And fast. If Jaci could pull the strings necessary to get her on the payroll and certified, then

Katie was all for it. It would be fun to work with Jaci and help make people prettier.

"Then it's, like, settled and stuff. But we're gonna have to change your name. Katie is too boring. I think you should be Kaci. Then we can be Jaci and Kaci. It rhymes."

Katie swallowed hard as she considered those possibilities. Yes, she supposed she could do that. And Kaci did sound like a hotter name. It sounded like the kind of a name a party girl bimbo would have. And that was basically Katie now. She loved to go out and pick up guys to take home with her. She loved to dance and flirt. Yes, Kaci made a lot of sense."

"I'll do it," Kaci announced.

"Oh goodie," Jaci called out as she once again wrapped her friend up in a hug. "You're gonna love it here."

It all happened so fast. Kaci was introduced to Johnny. He was excited about bringing her on. There was even an expedited class she could take that would get her certified in almost no time at all. Kaci could not wait.

The class was hard, but Kaci used every ounce of her stamina and intelligence to pass with top marks. She was the best in her class. She spent long days at the beauty school, which really cut into her ability to enjoy herself, but she knew it would all be worth it. It helped that Jaci would go out with her on the weekends, that was when they were not in the salon, having Kaci practice all the new skills she had learned in the past week.

By the time Kaci graduated beauty school, she was certain to be the best stylist she could possibly be. And those weekends spent practicing had somehow managed to make Kaci and Jaci look even more like each other. They sported the same long nails, painted pink. It was a good thing Kaci did not need to type anymore, because her nails would have made those sorts of activities almost impossible. But even their facial structure seemed to have merged until they were almost interchangeable.

But there was one difference that remained between them.

"To celebrate graduating," Jaci said, unable to keep herself from giggling, "it's time to complete your initiation."

Kaci was confused, not knowing what her friend meant, but she had an idea. Something had happened to Jaci to make her giggly and almost brainless. But Jaci had never shared what it was. Now it was Kaci's turn to join her.

There was a part of her that was worried. If she turned herself into an exact copy of Jaci, she would be dooming her life to that of a bimbo forevermore. There would be no going back. But the truth was, Kaci longed for her remaining worries to disappear. She envied Jaci. She wanted to be even more like her. They looked alike, other than the intelligence that still resided in Kaci's eyes, but otherwise they were interchangeable.

Kaci took a deep breath, letting the air out of her lungs slowly. "I'm ready."

Jaci took charge. She pulled Kaci into the back room. That was where they did the tattoo and piercing work that required more privacy. Kaci laid back on the table and Jaci pulled the future bimbo's skirt up. Kaci was not wearing any panties. But in this case, she did not need them.

"You won't have to sleep this one off," Jaci said as she prepared the piercing gun. "It's, like, super fast."

Kaci nodded her head, giving her friend the go ahead. She could not see what Jaci was doing, her own tits getting in the way, but she could feel the way her clit was getting pinched. Then there was a tiny jolt of pain. And then…

Kaci felt her mind go flat. There had been thoughts there a moment ago, but then there was nothing. She giggled, not knowing how she was supposed to react. Was it done?

"All done," Jaci announced. "Ooh, I love how empty your eyes look."

"And I'm going to love fucking what's left of her brains out," came the deep masculine voice of Johnny.

Kaci looked up at him and smiled. Then she giggled, not

entirely sure how she should react. She felt funny. She felt really good, but it was different. It was weird not having normal thoughts. But Kaci happily spread her legs wider, giving Johnny access to her most intimate place.

The moment his cock entered her pussy, her whole body sang out in erotic pleasure. Her nerves lit up all across her body with orgasmic energy. The euphoria she had felt before from sex was ten times more intense. Even if she was still capable of independent thought, there was no hope of that abasing the onslaught of pleasure that coursed through her body.

"Oh fuck," she called, the last intelligible sounds she would be making until Johnny had finished with her. After that, all she could do was moan, her plump lips hanging open, her head lulling to the side, drool starting to pool on the table. It was complete.

And then when Kaci came, when Johnny flooded her pussy with a torrent of cum, her body convulsed beneath him, the orgasmic pleasure searing through her, leaving nothing in its wake. All she felt was pleasure and happiness. There was nothing left inside of her.

Kaci had no concept of time while she recovered from having the last of her brains fucked out. The last piercing had hooked up her pleasure centers of her brain directly with her clit and pussy. It left her basically thinking with her cunt. That was all that was left to guide her.

Deep down, Kaci was still a functioning member of society. She could drive and she remembered every detail from her beauty school training, but her ability to learn anything new had almost been completely eliminated. She was stuck in this moment in time for the rest of her life. But it was the sexiest moment she could imagine.

"Like, thanks so much and stuff," Kaci said once she was able to sit up and think straight. Or at least she was thinking as straight as was possible with her bimbofied mind. "I feel, like, totally better now."

Jaci stepped up and kissed Kaci on the lips, their tongues snaking in and out of each other's mouths. They were identical in almost every way, truly interchangeable.

And when Jaci and Kaci walked back out onto the salon floor, their short skirts swishing around the tops of their thighs, their high heels clacking against the tile flooring, and their tits bouncing in their tight tops, they got to work, not caring which of the two customers that were scheduled they worked with.

Jaci or Kaci? It did not matter. They were two interchangeable bimbos. But there were two more salon chairs, two more employees they needed to find. Who would be joining them next?

JOINING BIMBODOM

Lorelei walked into the salon, not knowing what to expect. She had reached out to her friends, Jacki and Katie, letting them know that she was going to be in town for a couple weeks for business. Their friendship went way back, but she rarely got to see them anymore.

However, before she had even agreed to meet with them, it became clear that something had changed with her two friends. Instead of going by their usual names, they had decided to change their names to Jaci and Kaci. Lorelei had not expected that. It seemed unlike the women she had previously called her friends.

But both Jaci and Kaci seemed excited to see her. That could not be overlooked. And she knew it would be good to see them too, even if they had changed.

Walking into the salon, Lorelei had expected to find her friends as she had previously known them. They might have changed the name they wanted to be called, but Lorelei had assumed they had not changed that much. Instead, she found herself looking at two nearly identical bimbos. The blonde hair, the plump lips, the big tits, and the skimpy clothes all screamed bimbo to her.

"Lorelei," one of them squealed.

Before she knew it, Lorelei was in the tight embrace of both women. They had minced over to her on their impossibly high heels and then wrapped her into a tight hug, pressing their large chests into her, their tits pliant, yet firm, highlighting the fact that they were fake.

Lorelei was left asking what had happened to her two friends. She had no idea which woman was which. They looked so similar and so different from the women she remembered. Not that they looked bad. Even Lorelei had to admit that Jaci and Kaci looked good. They were hot and exuded sexuality with every fiber of their being. They were sex on heels and they left Lorelei feeling a little jealous of them.

"How?" Lorelei managed to ask. "Why?"

Those were the two major questions running through her mind. How had her friends changed so much? And why had they decided to turn themselves into almost perfect copies of each other. If it were not for how they had embraced her, she never would have figured that these two women were her friends. Although now that she had seen them, the change of their names made far more sense. They had bimbo names to match their bimbo bodies.

"It's fun," the other woman answered. Her plump lips were right next to Lorelei's ear, lightly blowing on her as her soft voice cooed.

Lorelei felt a shiver travel down her spine, lodging itself right in her core. She had never been someone who had much interest in other women, except for that one time in college when she did a little experimentation with her roommate, but the way sex just seemed to drip off of her two friends made it all but impossible to ignore them. They were just so hot and they seemed to promise unheard of levels of pleasure with every movement and every word spoken.

"Let's get her in a chair," the first woman said.

"Good idea, Jaci," the second woman answered.

Lorelei struggled to think under the onslaught of her friends' actions, but she could now start to put it all together. Jaci was the woman on her right. She wore a bright pink top that left a deep valley of cleavage on display. Kaci was on her left. She had been the one to coo into Lorelei's ear. She wore a midnight blue top that did not even close all the way in front of her chest. It was clear she was not wearing a bra. And both women wore short skirts that left all of their legs on display.

However, before Lorelei could even think to struggle against her friends' actions, she found herself being pulled into one of the four salon chairs available. And it was definitely a comfortable chair, possibly the most comfortable salon chair she had ever sat in before. She found her body naturally relaxing, finding comfort she was not aware she needed.

Traveling was hard sometimes. Lorelei had really started to feel that lately. When she was younger, the traveling was fun. Her life had been a constant adventure. But as time went on, she more and more discovered the downsides. Eating out every night left her with a little more around the middle than she liked. And she was never fully aware of what time zone she was in. Time in general had lost some of its meaning. Not to mention the frequent air travel was rough on her skin. She was constantly dehydrated.

"So what do you think, Kaci?" Jaci asked as they both assessed Lorelei. "Do you think blonde would look good on her?"

"Blonde?" Lorelei asked, her mind slow to keep up with the conversation. It was so difficult when all she wanted to do was sit back and relax.

"Blonde it the best," Kaci answered, running her hands through Lorelei's dark hair. "Much more fun than this."

Lorelei had never considered another hair color before. She had always been happy with her dark brown locks. But she had seen coworkers with blonde hair, some even bordering on platinum blonde, and she had to admit the color had looked good. The women seemed to smile more too. So did the people around them.

"What do you say?" Jaci asked as she leaned down and whispered into Lorelei's ear, once again causing a delicious shiver of pleasure to travel down to her core. Lorelei was getting far too turned on for something so basic as a reunion with her friends.

"Don't you want to see what it's like to be a blonde?" Kaci added, whispering into Lorelei's other ear.

Lorelei looked up into the mirror and saw her two friends flanking her. They both looked so hot. And their blonde hair did look fantastic. She figured this had to have been a change a long time coming, because they both had such long hair. Katie had always kept her hair short, so Lorelei was certain they had been building toward this moment for a long time.

"Of course she does," Jaci cooed. "Don't you want to know what it's like to have more fun?"

Jaci and Kaci went back and forth like that, turning Lorelei on all the while. And after a while, Lorelei could only agree with them. Yes, she wanted to find out what it was like to have blonde hair. She wanted to find out if the old adage of blondes having more fun was true. It certainly seemed that way given her friends' new proclivities, but there was only one way to know for sure.

"Yes, dye my hair blonde," Lorelei finally said. Her voice was weak, barely able to speak up. The rest of her attention was between her thighs. She ground them together, trying to keep her hands away from her pussy. She had no idea what her friends had planned for her, but she was about to find out.

As Jaci and Kaci got to work, they turned Lorelei away from the mirror so that she could not watch them work. It took hours, but Lorelei had nowhere else to be. And while it was a little weird seeing how her friends now looked and talked, they were actually more friendly than she remembered them being before. And for the first time in a long time, Lorelei felt completely relaxed. After her long flight across the country, relaxation was exactly what she needed.

But when those hours were complete, when Jaci spun Lorelei's chair around to face the mirror, Lorelei let out a gasp as she saw her new hair color for the first time. It was not just blonde. It was platinum blonde. She had never imagined her hair could be so light. But even though the change was massive, Lorelei could not help but smile. It looked good. The change would take time to get used to, but if her hair could remain healthy, Lorelei planned to remain blonde for the foreseeable future.

"That's amazing," Lorelei said, still focused on her hair. She turned her head this way and that, making sure she could see herself from every possible angle. She knew her boss would be in for a shock when he saw her next, but there was nothing in the company handbook that said she could not color her hair like this.

However, Jaci and Kaci, while smiling, were looking at each other with another idea passing unspoken between them. They had each gone through a similar step when they went blonde. Now it was time to let Lorelei in on the secret too.

"There's something else we want to do," Kaci said, once again cooing into Lorelei's ears. Both bimbos had learned how to manipulate people. It was how they managed to get by in the world. They were too sex obsessed to be considered smart anymore. They were too easily distracted. But when it came to getting something they wanted, like sex or sexy clothes, they could use their bodies and the promise of sex to get almost anything they wanted.

"Yeah?" Lorelei found herself asking without even realizing it. Her curiosity was piqued, even if she was still too caught up in her new appearance to fully notice.

"We want to pierce your belly-button," Jaci said, sending another jolt of pleasure down Lorelei's spine.

Lorelei took a deep breath, trying to center herself and get beyond the color change of her hair so that she could think more clearly. She felt inundated with pleasure. Her panties were soaked, her desire getting the better of her. Her arousal had snuck up on her. She had not expected to end up so turned on from a meeting with her friends. She had not expected to feel this way after relaxing in their wonderful salon chair and having her hair dyed.

"I don't know," Lorelei said, trying to figure out a reason why she should not get the piercing her friends were so intent on giving her. "I'm not really a piercing type of person."

And that was mostly true. Lorelei only had her ears pierced. She had never considered anything else. She had never wanted anything else. Not that Lorelei was against piercings in general. She saw how her friends looked. She could see the jewelry hanging from their belly-buttons. She could see the pink studs in their tongues when they opened their mouths. And she could even see the barbells in their nipples through their tight tops. She could not see their other significant piercing, but she was not ready for that yet.

"Come on," Kaci begged. "You'll look so pretty with a little extra bling."

"It won't even hurt that much," Jaci added. "We're like experts at this sort of thing. You totally need to trust us."

"I appreciate the work on my hair," Lorelei said, not wanting to cause a problem with her friends, "but I don't really think that's for me. I mean, I don't exactly have the figure to show off that sort of thing. You both do, obviously, but I can't do it."

"You don't have to show it off," Kaci cooed, getting right in Lorelei's ear again. "But you'll know it's there and feel sexier for it. Trust us."

Lorelei went stiff as Kaci continued her light blowing on her ear. And when Jaci joined in, echoing Kaci by saying, "Trust us," there was little that she could do. Between the pressure from her friends and her own arousal, Lorelei had no hope. She gave in, caving to the peer pressure, trying to argue with herself that if she did not like it, she could always just remove it and let it heal over.

"Oh goodie," both Jaci and Kaci squealed when Lorelei gave her consent. They quickly got to work, making sure to do everything by the book. Although, unlike when they usually pierced a customer's belly-button, the process with Lorelei was a little different. She was getting a special piercing, the same kind that they themselves had gotten as they started their transformations. Lorelei had no way of knowing that, but they were certain she was going to enjoy the results.

After spending her evening with Jaci and Kaci, getting her hair dyed blonde and having her belly-button pierced, Lorelei went straight to her hotel and quickly fell asleep. She came out early to see her friends, wanting to prepare for her boss to join her in advance of the meetings they would both be taking as they attempted to increase business for the company they worked for.

But when Lorelei woke up the next morning, she immediately knew that something was wrong. Or, maybe not wrong, but definitely different. She could just sense it.

Lorelei was used to waking up in unfamiliar places. She traveled enough to have already adapted to waking up in hotel rooms. She had managed to pull the shades completely closed, blocking out all light. But one glance at the bedside clock was enough to tell her that it was already morning.

If it was not the strange room, then what was different? That was the question Lorelei asked herself as she sat up and pulled her feet out from under the covers. She still did not feel it as she padded over to the window and threw open the curtains. She squinted against the incoming light, her view unremarkable, just a parking lot and a freeway beyond it. Not that she cared about the view. And she had seen worse in her life on the road.

It was only when Lorelei made it into the bathroom that she spotted what was wrong. It was the way her pajamas hung off her body. Her years on the road, of always eating restaurant meals and sitting for long periods on airplanes had left her with a spread around the middle that she disliked, but had never been able to avoid. But now it was gone.

Lorelei raised her pajama top, exposing her midriff, to discover that not only had the inches simply melted away overnight, but that she now had a tight and toned torso that made it look like she spent hours in the gym every week.

"Wow," Lorelei gasped as she pulled up her top further. It was not just the area around her middle. Her whole body had slimmed down, giving her an athletic look that she had never had before.

Lorelei slowly stripped down until she was nude. She was still coming to terms with the change in her hair color, but now her body was giving her second thoughts as well. None of it made sense. How did it happen?

Before Lorelei did anything else, she phoned Jaci, hoping she and Kaci could provide an answer. In setting up their meeting the night before, she had learned that the two friends were now also roommates, so she knew if she called one of them, she could probably get an answer. However, her friends seemed less than helpful. They mostly giggled as Lorelei tried to ask her questions. And it did not help that there was so much moaning going on in the background.

It was only after Lorelei had given up with the call and hung up that she realized what those moans were. One or both of her friends had been having sex. She had interrupted them. That explained why they did not have much in the way of answers for her, but it was still shocking for her. Lorelei was not a prude, but she also did not have the same openness that her friends now seemed to both share. It was going to take time for her to adjust to their changes, just as it would take time for her to adjust to her changes.

"What am I going to wear?" Lorelei finally asked herself as she looked through her suitcase. It quickly became apparent that she had nothing that would fit her new frame. It was a small miracle her pajama pants had managed to stay up as she moved around the hotel room. She had lost some of the mass on her hips, although not as much as the rest of her weight loss would have indicated.

It was only after Lorelei had showered, deciding it was best to put off figuring out what she was going to wear that she got a text from Jaci telling her that her friends were going to take her out shopping. It seemed their sex-filled morning was finally over. And they promised to bring her clothing to wear.

"Hey, babe," Jaci said as she entered Lorelei's room and gave her friend a hug.

"You're looking so hot," Kaci said a moment later, giving Lorelei a similar hug.

It was not long before Lorelei was dressed. When Jaci and Kaci had promised to bring clothing, she had assumed they would bring her slutty clothes like they wore with drastically low necklines and tiny skirts. But Lorelei could almost consider the clothing normal. Yes, the top was cropped, but given how good she now looked with her tight midriff and the pink barbell in her belly-button, she felt more like showing it off. Since she now had it, she might as well flaunt it.

The day turned into a whirlwind of shopping and other fun. Lorelei quickly came to understand that her friends really were bimbos through and through. Her first experience with them had not been a fluke. But she also had to admit they both seemed happy and for the first time in a long time, Lorelei felt completely free of pressure. That would change tomorrow when her boss was set to arrive, but in the meantime, she could enjoy herself.

Interspersed between bouts of shopping, the three friends stopped for drinks. That only seemed to make the day more fun. Lorelei never got drunk, but the alcohol certainly helped take the edge off and made it easier for her to let Jaci and Kaci to take charge.

Therefore it might have been a bit of a surprise that Lorelei found herself back at the salon where she had met her friends the night before.

"Why are we here?" Lorelei asked. She was mostly sober, but she still felt a little lightheaded. Her outfit had not really changed. Her purchases had included lots of midriff baring tops and tight fitting bottoms, both pants and skirts. She purchased a whole new skirt suit for work, including a fitted white blouse that hugged her body. A tailor had been needed to bring in the jacket and skirt to fit her body properly, something that had been rare for her before. If anything, her work outfits usually had to be let out to fit her.

But now that they were back at the salon, Jaci and Kaci were ready to push Lorelei into the next step. Lorelei flopped down into a salon chair, happy to rest and relax after the fun day they had spent together. However, that only gave her friends time to prepare.

"What are you doing?" Lorelei asked as Jaci wheeled a cart over with the piercing gun and other supplies.

"You look so hot already, but we think you could be even hotter," Kaci cooed.

Lorelei felt soft hands on her shoulders, pressing her down into the chair. She tried to struggle, but Kaci's strength was too much for her. Lorelei slumped back.

"What did you have in mind?" Lorelei finally asked. She did not really understand how she had lost weight overnight, but she was not complaining. If Lorelei had truly stopped to consider the cause, it would have been obvious, even if it did not make sense. It was the belly-button piercing that had done it through some strange kind of magic or technology. Lorelei had no way of knowing. But that should have made her suspicious of what her friends had in store for her next.

"You'd look totes hot with a tongue stud," Kaci pressed, cooing in Lorelei's ear, just like last night. Lorelei felt as if there had been a wire connected directly from her ear to her pussy. All it took was the most simple of actions by Kaci and Lorelei was a gushing mess, more than ready for some sexual fun.

"I can't," Lorelei complained as she tried to sit up straight. Except with Kaci's hands still on her shoulders and with her still sitting in the comfortable chair, there was little that Lorelei could do.

"Of course you can," Kaci continued. "You'll be so cute with a little bit of pink in your mouth, just like Jaci and me."

Lorelei looked up into the mirror and watched as both her friends licked their lips, their pink tongue studs darting out from between their plump lips.

"No, you don't get it," Lorelei continued. "I have to be able to talk for my job. I can't have a lisp or get stuck mumbling. My job depends on it."

"Babe," Jaci said as she placed a calming hand on Lorelei's thigh. "It'll be totally fine. You'll see. And just imagine how good it will be to kiss with a little bit of metal in your mouth."

Jaci and Kaci turned toward each other and began to kiss each other. Lorelei's eyes locked onto the scene playing out in the mirror, unable to look away. She was hot and aroused before, but seeing her friends make out amped up her arousal even higher. Her core felt as if it was melting, the heat becoming more than she could handle.

"Yes, okay, I'll do it."

Lorelei did not know why she agreed to let her friends pierce her tongue, but she simply could not hold back against the onslaught of sexual feelings coursing through her body. The energy in the room was palpable and the only way she was going to find relief was if she gave into her friends' demands. She would get the tongue stud, crossing her fingers that it did not jeopardize her job in any way.

Jaci made quick work of the situation. She pulled out a pair of forceps and held tight to Lorelei's tongue. Kaci took hold of the piercing gun and performed the deed, piercing a hole through Lorelei's tongue. A moment later, there was a bright pink stud sticking through the hole. Lorelei had a tongue piercing now.

The pain had been minimal. So too had the pain for her belly-button. And if Lorelei did not know better, she would have recognized that the piercing was different from what she had expected. So too were the results.

However, as Lorelei sat there, letting her friends dote on her, she found a surge of tiredness hit her. She yawned, unable to keep her mouth closed. She was very aware that her yawn placed the bright pink stud in her tongue on display, but she could not help herself. Lorelei figured that she was feeling the travel. Yesterday had been a long day. Now her boss was set to arrive in the morning and it only made sense to get a good night's sleep.

Lorelei bid her friends adieu and returned to her hotel for the night. She slipped out of her clothes and climbed under the covers, not even thinking about the fact she was about to sleep in the nude. But before she could consider that fact, she was asleep, her head resting peacefully on the pillow, a smile tugging at her lips.

CHAPTER 3

Lorelei was not surprised when she woke up and discovered that her lips had plumped up overnight. After seeing her friends with similar lips, she was no longer surprised by such things. And if Lorelei was honest with herself, she liked how her new lips looked on her. They made her feel sexy in a way she had never felt before. It was new and very much welcome.

Everything that had happened to Lorelei since she arrived in town had been wonderful. She had a sexy body and now she had a sexy face to go along with it. But even though so much had changed for her, it was not time to buckle down and go to work. Lorelei's boss had arrived at the hotel an hour earlier and he wanted to get started as soon as he had time to freshen up. Lorelei was to meet him in his room to begin going over the plan for the next few days.

Knocking on her boss' door, Lorelei shifted uncomfortably from one foot to the other. She was unsure what he would say when he saw the new her. It was one thing to dye her hair, but the rest of the changes to her body were rather more difficult to explain. It had only been a few days since they last saw each other. Surely her boss would have questions about why she looked so different.

"Lorelei?" her boss asked as he opened the door to find his employee standing in front of him. His jaw nearly hit the floor as he took her in for the first time.

"Yes, sir," Lorelei answered. But referring to him as sir was the oddest of responses. In all her working life, she had never called her boss sir before. He had always been Seth or Mr. Tyson before. But as the word slipped from her lips, she could not help but feel that it accurately described him and their relationship. It felt natural to call him that.

"Please, come in," he said, beckoning her forward, unwilling to question her new look. Whatever she had done, he approved.

Lorelei followed her boss into his room, but as soon as the door closed behind her, she dropped to her knees. She had not planned this, but now that she was here, she could not see herself doing anything else. As much as she liked the look of her newly plumped lips, there was a deep need to put those lips to use. Therefore, it was with deft fingers that she reached up and unbuckled her boss' belt. He looked on in shocked silence as she freed his cock.

The moment her lips were wrapped around his hard shaft, it felt as if everything were right with the world. Lorelei felt a sense of fulfillment that she had never experienced before. Her day with her friends had felt amazing, but this easily topped that. It was like Lorelei was meant to be on her knees. She was meant to sit at her boss's feet and suck on his cock.

And even if her boss wanted to protest, there was no way he could deny himself the pleasure Lorelei now provided him. There was only one way for the moment to end and that was with him cumming down Lorelei's throat.

It did not take long. Seeing the new and improved Lorelei was enough to make him ready. His cock surged and he sent a flood of cum into her mouth and down her throat. Lorelei lapped it up, loving the flavors as she swallowed down his cum. She loved the great groan of pleasure that he released as he gave her the reward for a job well done.

"Thank you, sir," Lorelei said once she had finished, once his cock was safely back in its place. There was a smile on her face and a contentment in her posture that could not be faked. She had never been happier.

Seth Tyson avoided asking what happened to Lorelei for the rest of the day. He was curious. He was definitely curious. But there was no way he could ask her what had happened without breaking some unspoken rule about a woman's body. He felt embarrassed to have even thought the question. And even if he had been able to ask it, Lorelei had no satisfactory answer. She could guess and she wanted to ask her friends about the changes she had undergone, but it was almost like she was afraid to ask. Asking the question might make her revert back to her former self and there was no way Lorelei could stand for that. She loved everything about the changes she had undergone.

Lorelei especially liked the way her lips kept ending up wrapped around her boss' cock. Her morning blowjob was not the only one she gave him that day. Deep down, she knew that there was no way she should be behaving this way. There was no way her new piercings could have healed so quickly. And yet, there was no pain, there was no discomfort, and even if she had been told to refrain from blowing her boss, it was impossible for her to avoid it. It was a desire she could not explain, but was happy to give into every time it reared its head.

But after a full day preparing with her boss for the meetings that would take place for the rest of the week, Lorelei left her boss to rest in his hotel room, having once again sucked a creamy load from his cock, so that she could meet up with her friends. She wanted to spend as much time with Jaci and Kaci as she could, knowing that her time in town, even though it was supposed to span weeks, would be limited.

"So kissable," Jaci said in greeting as Lorelei stepped into the salon. Kaci was still in the back, finishing with the last customer of the day, providing a piercing that required privacy.

To emphasize the point, Jaci pushed her substantial tits into Lorelei's chest and pressed her plump lips to Lorelei's own. The pair open mouth kissed, fully enjoying themselves, their tongues dancing in each other's mouths.

"Mmm, that was nice," Lorelei said when Jaci finally broke the kiss. Her eyes looked distant, still lost in the pleasure that was left over from the sexy kiss. Lorelei had never really considered herself interested in women before this, but now she could safely say that she was entirely bisexual. Men, women, it did not matter. And since her friends were so incredibly sexy, it only made sense to make out with them when the opportunity presented itself. Lorelei was past the point where she could judge them.

It was only a minute later when a sexy coed from the local university stumbled out of the backroom. Lorelei had no idea what piercing the woman had chosen, but the way her eyes looked hazy and distant, she could guess that Kaci had given the woman a little extra attention. A nice orgasm would be wonderful.

"Let's get you back there now," Jaci said once the previous customer had left the salon.

"What?" Lorelei asked, confused. "But I'm not getting anything more done."

A knowing smile appeared on Jaci's face. It was as if the argument had already been won and Lorelei was just delaying the inevitable.

"You say that now, but just wait a little while," Jaci pressed. "By the end of the night, you'll be feeling pretty silly. You'll be feeling as silly as Kaci and me."

Lorelei did not know what to say to that, but it did not matter, because Kaci appeared a moment later, stepping out of the backroom and embracing Lorelei in the same manner that Jaci had before. Lorelei melted into Kaci's kiss, finding jolts of tingling pleasure shooting into her core, making her hotter and more aroused than ever before.

Time lost meaning as Lorelei found herself being slowly led into the backroom. She was putty in her friends' hands, unable and unwilling to push back against the steady pressure to be more and more like them.

"I'm not a bimbo," Lorelei managed to mumble, but that only elicited giggles from her friends. They both gave her a look that seemed to say, "Not yet," but it made her feel like she was not far from joining them.

When Kaci and Jaci finally let Lorelei catch her breath, she found herself sitting in a reclining chair in the middle of the backroom. Her suit jacket was open and several buttons on her blouse had been undone, revealing both her upper chest and the lacy white bra she wore underneath it.

When the trio went out shopping the day before, they had tried to get Lorelei to skip the bra shopping. She had not seen either of them wear a bra since she arrived, but with their big and obviously fake tits, there did not seem to be much need. But Lorelei had insisted. She had moved to buy several at the lingerie store that had sized her, but when she actually made it back to her hotel room with her purchases, all but this one bra had disappeared. They were not even listed on her receipts.

Lorelei would have protested about the way her friends were slowly stripping her, but she had to admit that it felt good. She was just so hot, her skin making it feel like she was on fire with arousal. It turned out that kissing her friends had only made her arousal situation worse. And it was not like she had orgasmed for a while. Working all day with her boss, sacrificing her own pleasure for his, had left her wet and more than ready for some sexy fun.

"I'm so horny," Lorelei complained, her voice coming out as a moan. Her hands pushed down her body reaching toward the junction between her legs. Her below knee length skirt was in the way, but she could not help herself. She was so turned on and wanted nothing more than to cum.

Jaci and Kaci looked at each other and giggled. They knew that this was their moment.

"We can help you, but you need to do something for us first," Jaci said.

"What?" Lorelei asked, her eyes lidded with lust.

"Let us pierce your nipples," Kaci answered excitedly. She already had the tray with the piercing gun ready. The jewelry was ready. Lorelei just needed to give her permission.

"But—"

"No buts," Jaci interrupted. "Just think how sexy you'll be with a little bit of jewelry in your nipples."

"And how good it will feel when we lick them," Kaci added.

Lorelei shuddered as she imagined just that. She had never been someone who cared about pierced nipples or pierced anything else, but now that she had seen her friends like this, now that she had experienced what it was like to have a pierced belly-button and a pierced tongue, she was beginning to come around to their way of thinking. It was sexy. She was already sexy, but Lorelei knew she had so much further to go. Jaci and Kaci were feminine perfection in her eyes and their pierced nipples looked so sexy under their tight tops.

"But what about my job?" Lorelei asked, grabbing at whatever straws of thought she could manage to develop against the peer pressure from her friends.

"No one has to know," Jaci lied. Both Jaci and Kaci knew what would happen when Lorelei got her nipples pierced. No one would miss the massive change in her figure. But they were both confident that Lorelei would begin to see things their way once it was done.

Another wave of heat passed through the helpless businesswoman. She did not even know what caused it, but she knew she could not stand it for much longer. If she did not get relief soon, she would go crazy.

"Okay," Lorelei finally relented. "Do it. Pierce my nipples."

Jaci finished unbuttoning Lorelei's blouse and then stripped her upper body completely. Kaci finished preparing for the piercing. Everyone was grinning, even Lorelei, although she had no idea what was about to happen to her.

CHAPTER 4

"Holy fuck, these are tits," Lorelei practically screamed as she woke up the next morning. She had gone to bed as soon as she returned to the hotel, finding herself far more tired than she had expected. But now that she was awake, she was faced with the fact she now sported tits that were equal in size and shape to her friends.

Jumping out of bed, Lorelei ran into the bathroom to get a view of herself and her new tits. They were big, completely dominating her frame. And when coupled with the blonde hair and plump lips, there was only one possible outcome. Lorelei looked like a bimbo.

Not knowing what to do with herself, Lorelei tried to go about her day as it had been planned. There was no way she could wear her new bra with her new tits. That was just a recipe for pain. But there were other problems too. The work blouses she had previously purchased to fit her thinner frame no longer fit. They were fine as she buttoned them up, but as soon as she reached her chest, she was stuck, the two sides of the fabric refusing to meet in the middle.

To make matters worse, Lorelei did not have a jacket that covered her chest either. Everything she owned that was business appropriate was now fitted to her frame, but without the large tits bolted onto her chest. She had thrown away her old clothes, happy to see them gone. Now she was regretting it.

When Lorelei finally left her room, needing to meet her boss before their first prospective client meeting of the day, there was no way to hide what had happened. Seth Tyson's eyes bugged out the moment he saw her in the lobby. He had never seen such an appetizing view of cleavage before, but it made it even harder considering that he needed Lorelei to look professional today. And no matter what she did, there was no way she could play that role.

"What happened to you?" her boss asked. He did not even give her a normal greeting. He went right to the heart of the matter.

Before Lorelei answered, she had to fight a sweeping need to drop to her knees and give her boss a blowjob. It seemed being in a public lobby was not enough to prevent her from feeling such an urge. But even as Lorelei steeled herself against her body's desires, she could not get past the fact she had no explanation for the change in her appearance.

"I can't explain it, sir," she finally answered. "I just woke up like this and none of my clothes fit me right anymore."

Her boss took a deep breath, his eyes never once leaving her tits, as he tried to think of a solution. "Some of these people are very conservative and they may not like this look you have going, the sexy secretary look I'll call it, but it's too late to do anything about it now. We've got appointments to keep."

Lorelei found herself to be the center of attention as soon as they stepped into their first meeting. Half the people kept staring at her tits and the other half glared at her. She had wanted to try to explain why she looked the way she did, but there was no way any of them would believe that her friends persuading her to get her nipples pierced had led to her having big, fake tits.

But it all went downhill from there. Lorelei's boss did most of the talking, leaving her to just sit there. But when it became clear that this first meeting of the day was turning into a bust, Lorelei grew desperate. She did the only thing that felt natural in the situation. She propositioned the CEO sitting across from her, offering herself up in exchange for him signing the contract.

Lorelei did not do this in public. The CEO had stepped out for a moment and Lorelei had given an excuse to leave the meeting as well. When she caught up to the CEO in a secluded hallway, she put on all the charm that she could.

"You know, I think there's a way we can still make this deal work," she said, fluttering her eyelashes as she placed a soft hand on the man's arm. "I will do anything to get us across the line. I think you'll find that I can be exceptionally persuasive."

It almost seemed like it would work. Lorelei could not believe she was doing it, but she did not see another option. She blamed herself for failing to secure the contract. If only she had not given in and gotten her nipples pierced, the deal would have been a breeze.

However, rather than become flattered or enamored with Lorelei's offer, the CEO's expression hardened. His indifference toward her turned to anger.

"How dare you?" he shouted. "Get out of my building you harlot."

Lorelei's boss came running, hearing the commotion outside. It only took him a moment to put everything together, to know what Lorelei had done.

"Lorelei, you're fired."

And just like that, Lorelei was jobless and stranded over a

thousand miles from her home. Dejected, she walked out, only realizing afterward that the CEO she had just propositioned was also a religious leader who had taken a vow of chastity. Sure, he could have been corrupt. There were plenty of religious figures who were, but that had not been Lorelei's luck. She had propositioned the wrong man and now she had paid for it with her job. Worse, she was horny and needed to find some relief.

There was only one place for Lorelei to go after that. She went straight to the salon where her friends worked. She knew they would be busy with customers, but there was nowhere else for her to go. She could return to her hotel room, but that felt wrong, since she had just been fired and the room had been paid for by the company. She would return to get her belongings eventually, but first she needed some sympathy.

"Wow, you're looking like a real hot babe," Kaci said when Lorelei walked into the salon. It did not matter that Lorelei felt in the dumps, just seeing her friend in all her bimbo happiness healed to raise her spirits.

"Thanks, but I got fired."

"Oh no," Kaci said, mincing over in her high heels and wrapping Lorelei into a hug. "But don't worry. You can come work here. Johnny is looking for another girl like us."

"But I'm not a hair stylist or tattoo artist like you two," Lorelei complained. However, as she stood there with Kaci's arms wrapped around her, she had to admit, there was a certain attraction to living and working like her friends. Maybe it was the arousal talking, but the whole idea of living a bimbo life sounded really good. But there was still the lack of training.

"Johnny can set you up," Kaci said. "He did that for me and stuff. And now I'm like an expert or something. It's all kind of confusing, but I know all that I'm, like, supposed to know."

"I guess I can consider it," Lorelei said, her mind whirring with possibilities. Could she really give up the travel and the corporate job and do something as simple as style hair and the rest? Was it really that easy?

"Yay," Kaci exclaimed, not bothered by the fact that Lorelei had not actually agreed yet. She let go of Lorelei and turned toward Jaci who was finishing up with a customer's hair. "Jaci, Laci is going to join us."

Lorelei's eyes widened, both at the assumption that she was indeed joining them, but also in her being called Laci. She had never even considered such a name change. But even Lorelei had to admit that if she were to join her friends, the name change would make some degree of sense. They could be Jaci, Kaci, and Laci, a trio of bimbo friends.

Maybe it was getting to be closer to her friends. Maybe it was an opportunity that would let her get right back on her feet again. Or maybe it was her arousal clouding her thinking, but Lorelei had a sudden revelation.

"Yes, I'm going to do it," she announced, a big smile gracing her lips.

That announcement forever changed her life. Lorelei became Laci. It was surprisingly easy to adjust to the name change. By the end of the day, she was answering to Laci as if she had been called that all her life. She also got to meet Johnny. He welcomed her aboard and arranged for her to attend an expedited beauty school. Laci would go away for her new schooling, paid for by the salon, and then she would return for her final initiation. It was that simple.

But it was the final initiation that worried Laci. She loved her friends dearly and appreciated the fact that they had helped change her life for the better. And while she was away at beauty school, she found she really enjoyed the work. She was excited to return to the salon and make her full contribution.

Along the way, Laci had fully adapted to her body and the lifestyle her friends had pushed her toward. Sex was such a wonderful thing and Laci loved having it as often as possible. And even more than that, she had come to love showing off her sexy body. It was a rare day when someone did not find out what color panties she was wearing due to her short skirts or low-rising shorts, assuming she was wearing panties at all. Sometimes they just got in the way.

But even once Laci had returned to the salon for her first day, she knew there was still a big difference between her and her friends. There was something that truly separated them. Laci had retained her intelligence. She could act silly and dumb almost all the time, but there was still something ticking behind her eyes, something she could never hope to eliminate. She was not a true bimbo.

The initiation remained a secret even after Laci had returned and embraced her bimbo friends. It was difficult to tell them all apart now. Laci knew the difference between her two friends, but a stranger would not only struggle to pick out the differences between Jaci and Kaci, but with Laci as well. They were all almost identical, and almost interchangeable as well. Almost.

After the initial welcomes were finished, Laci found herself being beckoned into the backroom. Johnny was already there, waiting for her. And there was a piercing tray all ready to go. But she had no idea what to expect.

"Strip for me," Johnny said.

Without question, Laci started to take off her clothes. She had been prepared for the night to end with sex. Jaci and Kaci had both filled her in on some of the fun they had with Johnny. Laci had not yet had the opportunity, but she was definitely looking forward to it and had planned accordingly. She easily pulled the tube top she wore off, tossing it across the room without a care. Her skirt soon followed. All she was left wearing was her high heels, which she did not really plan to take off. She practically lived in heels now.

Laci climbed into the chair and placed her feet in the stirrups. She did not know why they had been brought out, but she was not about to argue or question. Her heart pounded in her chest as Jaci and Kaci stepped forward, the tools of their trade in their hands. Johnny placed a comforting hand on her shoulder as she closed her eyes.

The pinching of Laci's clit was the first thing she felt. Then there was a brief sting as the piercing gun did its work. And that was followed by the strangest sensation Laci had ever felt. She had always had the ability to channel her sexuality and mostly shut off her brain during sex. She was still there, even when she played the part of the sexy bimbo. But the piercing of her clit made it feel like Laci's brain had been cross wired. Her intelligence was shorted out. One moment it was there and then the next moment it was gone. This final piercing had immediate effect.

When Laci opened her eyes, there was no longer the spark of intelligence in them. She smiled at her friends, feeling nothing but lust and giggles.

"She's one of us," Kaci cheered, seeing the drastic change in Laci.

Kaci started what came next by bending low and kissing Laci's pussy. The newly formed bimbo moaned as pleasure shot through her body. Jaci was next, adding a little bit of tongue action into the kiss, making Laci's hips buck.

Laci gave a lust filled stare, a fire of need taking over her ability to think at all. All that was left in her, at least for the moment, was a need for sex. She needed to get fucked.

And for that, there was Johnny. He positioned himself between Laci's legs and thrust his hard cock into her without any extra fanfare. Laci screamed out as pleasure erupted all over her body. All it had taken was a single thrust to send her over the edge, plunging into a deep chasm of pleasure, her body almost convulsing as she came.

Jaci and Kaci joined in as Johnny set up a steady rhythm. They each took a side, bending low to take a nipple into each of their mouths. Laci had no way to remember which of them had told her how good she would feel with her nipples getting licked with their pierced tongues. It was even better when they took turns kissing Laci, letting their tongues dance as Laci built up for another epic orgasm.

Laci was in heaven, her body screaming out in pleasure. Her whole body felt as if it was on fire, but the heat only made her feel better. Not a single thought filtered through her lust addled mind. There was only the instinct of a bimbo remaining. What few thoughts she would be able to manage could come later, when she was not suffering from an overload of orgasmic pleasure. For now, all she could do was lay back and enjoy it.

Johnny's thrusts grew both in pace and severity. It did not take long before he pounded into his new employee, giving her all he could muster as he fucked her hard and fast. Even as Laci was lost to the pleasure, her body responded to the situation, milking his cock, enhancing his pleasure to make sure he gave her what she so dearly needed. And when he came, his cock surging with a torrent of cum, Laci came too. Her body convulsed and she called out, her mind completely inundated with pleasure.

When it was all over, it took Laci time to recover. She had never been fucked like that before. And when she fully returned to her senses, it took a moment for her to realize that she was now a slow and dimwitted bimbo. Her mind no longer had a higher gear to operate with. But as scary as that could have felt, Laci felt nothing but pride. She was a proper bimbo now. She and her friends were bimbos through and through. And being a bimbo was better than she ever could have imagined. She was ready to continue her life, having turned over a new leaf and truly become the embodiment of Laci the bimbo. This was who she was, now and forever.

But when Laci finally returned to the main room of the salon, when she was able to take up her proper spot, claiming one of the salon chairs as her own, she and the other bimbos were faced with a simple question. Who else was going to join them?

BIMBO SALON

Margot stepped into the salon, clothing her résumé to her chest. She had been searching for a job for weeks now, but with no luck in finding anything. There was always someone else with more experience or with better connections. The salons and parlors she had applied to always got back to her after the interview process had concluded and it was always the same story. They really liked her, but there was someone who was just a slightly better fit. Margot kept coming in second place.

However, the moment Margot stepped into this salon, she knew there was something different about it. There were three women working at the salon chairs, helping young women look their best. It seemed like a happy and bustling place. Although the moment Margot started comparing the three stylists hard at work, she noticed something strange about them. They looked almost identical. They were each bottle blondes with large breasts, plump lips, and bodies that looked like the Greek god Zeus had designed them for the purpose of sex.

That should have been enough for Margot to walk right out again. The women working looked almost interchangeable on top of the way they bared so much of their bodies. Low-cut crop tops and micro skirts seemed to be the work uniform they each wore, although in different colors. The insanely high heels did not help matters. They looked like they were walking on tall pedestals, not shoes.

However, Margot was only looking at half of the salon. The other half seemed to be devoted to tattoos and piercings. And it was that fact that had actually led her to seeing if there were any available jobs available. Not only had Margot passed beauty school, but she had also gone through and been trained as a tattoo artist and body piercer. She had always loved the idea of people using their bodies as a canvas for art, although that had not translated to her own use of those materials.

Margot was a simple woman. She enjoyed making other people look their best, but that came as a contrast to how she usually took care of herself. She took little care in her appearance, although she had recently had her hair bleached. Her intention was to dye it a completely unnatural color, like pink or blue, but in the meantime, it looked about as close to platinum blonde as was possible.

Not wanting to interrupt the three stylists working with their customers, Margot sat down in the empty waiting area. She surveyed the magazines on offer, finding a mix of glamor magazines and what could almost be considered fetish magazines. The magazines were all safe for work, but they were there to serve as inspiration for those looking to get tattoos or piercings.

Margot picked up one of the more fetish style magazines and started flipping through it. There were some interesting tattoos that some of the models had gotten, although all of them seemed to be of the tribal variety that she generally found to be too generic and without any meaning behind them. But they did look good. She tried to imagine herself with some of those tattoos, but she could not get over how wrong they would feel.

Looking up, Margot thought it would have made more sense for one of the stylists to have tribal style tattoos. She did not see any ink on their exposed skin—there was a lot of exposed skin —but they had the tanned and fit bodies that could have had such tattoos without anyone questioning them.

All three of the stylists finished with their customers at nearly the same time. Margot continued to wait, not wanting to interrupt their process. They each cleaned up their work stations before they collectively walked over to greet Margot. She had not come with an appointment. She probably should have, but she had been too nervous to call ahead, instead deciding to just drop in. If they wanted her to make an appointment to talk about employment, she could do that and come back. It was oddly easier that way.

"Hi there," the woman in the middle said with a smile on her face. Actually, all three women were smiling with almost identical smiles. Margot found it a little unnerving. The only differences she could spot between the three women was in their clothing. The woman who spoke wore a green top with a black skirt.The woman on the left wore a blue top and the woman on the right wore a red colored top.

The tops themselves, beyond color, looked identical. They had scooping necklines that highlighted the size and shape of their tits. And at their size, it felt proper to call them tits. They each had a similar set of fake looking tits that barely remained decent. Their midriffs were bare, revealing flat bellies, each of them sporting a pink stud in their belly-buttons. Their skirts were short and low-slung on their hips, leaving almost nothing to the imagination. A gust of wind or simply bending over a little would surely reveal their panties, assuming they were wearing any.

"Hi," Margot responded, standing up but still feeling dwarfed by the three women. Their high heels made them appear far taller. Margot wore a simple set of flats, although she had dressed up a little, wearing a button-up blouse and a nice pair of pants. She wanted to make a good impression, even if she could not even begin to compare herself to her potential coworkers. While they were hot, Margot was not. She was rounder than she wanted to be and her skin looked almost sickly pale. "My name is Margot. I saw the help wanted ad in the newspaper. Here's my résumé."

Margot held out her résumé to the three women, not sure which of them would want to look at it. She had not had a lot of success in holding down a job, despite her qualification. She kept ending up working at salons and parlors that ended up closing after she was hired. At her last job, the owner had died, leaving the business to close down. There was no one else to run the business.

The woman in blue reached out with a long-nailed hand, her nails colored a bright pink that matched her belly-button jewelry, and took the piece of paper. Her eyes went a little cross-eyed as she looked at the page, her lips moving as she silently sounded out the words. If Margot had not been so nervous, she would have questioned why the woman behaved that way. Did she really have that much trouble reading? Margot had never really considered that before, but then again, all three women looked like interchangeable bimbos. Reading probably was not their forte.

"She's perfect," the woman in blue finally said.

"Oh goodie," the woman in red said.

"If you want to be one of us, we can help," the woman in green said. She seemed to be the leader of the trio, although Margot could not tell them apart except by the color of tops they wore. "I'm Jaci and this is Kaci and Laci."

"Which is which?" Margot asked, thoroughly confused.

The women just giggled, all three of them. But then Jaci continued speaking, "You're résumé checks out. Let's have you sit in one of the chairs and relax. I just need to, like, check on something and stuff."

Margot nodded her head and allowed Kaci and Laci to lead her to the empty salon chair. It was the most comfortable salon chair she had ever sat in. It was both firm, but also soft, letting her sink down, all the tension in her body releasing all at once. She let out a long sigh, letting her eyes flutter before they closed entirely. The only sounds around her were the giggles of Kaci and Laci as they moved about the room, their heels clacking on the tiled floor.

When a third set of heels joined in, Margot opened her eyes again to find Jaci's smiling face. She knew it was Jaci because of the green top. "I just talked to Johnny. He owns the place. You're hired."

"I am?" Margot asked, almost too giddy to believe it. She had gone to countless job interviews, trying to find a job as a stylist or as a body piercer and tattoo artist for weeks. And now she had just gotten the job without even an interview? It did not make sense, but Margot was not about to argue the point.

"There's just one thing you've got to do first. We need to pierce your belly-button."

"You what?" Margot said, suddenly fearful as she sat up straight. She looked at the three women, hoping they were just pulling her leg, but even though they smiled at her, it was clear they were completely serious. She looked down at her rounded torso. She knew she should eat better and exercise, but it always seemed so hard. She already knew that a piercing like that would not look good on her. She did not have the abs for it. They were hidden beneath too many layers of fat.

"It's part of being one of us," the blue-topped woman said. "To work here you gotta look the part."

"Don't worry," the red-topped woman added. "It doesn't even really hurt and by tomorrow you'll totally understand. It'll, like, make so much sense and stuff."

Margot knew she was getting pressured to get the piercing. It was not the first time she had experienced peer pressure. But as she looked around the room, not just at her potential coworkers, but the salon itself, there was something about it that drew her in. She felt like this was a place she could work for a long time. She could make a career for herself at this salon. What was a little pain in the face of that? And it was not like she needed to keep the piercing in long term. She could take it out and let it heal as soon as she had fully secured the job.

"Okay, fine," Margot relented.

The three bimbo stylists cheered before they got to work. It was only minutes later that Margot's blouse had been rolled up, revealing her midriff and belly-button. The pink barbell they had given her looked out of place in Margot's eyes, but they seemed satisfied. Margot did not know what to say, except to thank them for the opportunity. She looked forward to meeting Johnny. But Margot was sent home and told to return tomorrow, for her second part of the initiation.

As Margot returned home, she questioned whether this job was worth the hoops she was having to jump through, but there was only so much she could think on the matter. No matter how much she felt strange about it all, she found herself yawning. The desire for sleep was overwhelming. As much as she wanted to celebrate getting a new job, she found herself crawling into bed as soon as she got home. And once her head hit the pillow, she was out like a light.

The moment Margot woke up, she knew something had changed. She could simply sense it, although as she still laid in bed, she could not diagnose what had actually changed. She just felt that there had been a change.

It was only after Margot had climbed out of bed and shuffled into her bathroom to start her day that she saw the way her pajamas hung off her body.

"Holy shit," she cried out with a surprised smile on her face. "I look amazing."

And she did. Margot had gone from overweight to having a tight and toned body, all without stepping a single foot inside a gym. She was ecstatic. And when she lifted her top to see the perfectly healed belly-button piercing, she smiled, knowing that somehow it was the cause of her sudden change in appearance.

Unfortunately, despite the killer body, Margot realized that not everything about her had changed. Her body looked great, but her clothing had not changed with her body. And she still had the same face, although with a little less volume in her cheeks. So while she loved the change, she now had no way to go out. And since she had been out of work recently, she did not have the money to buy new clothes, let alone a whole new wardrobe.

Not that a lack of clothes stopped Margot from going about her day as she had originally planned. And after a shower where she fully explored her new body, she was excited to see a message from Jaci. She seemed to already be aware of her clothing difficulties and as long as she could get herself to the salon, she and the other women would make sure she was taken care of. And Margot would have the opportunity to shadow them as they did their jobs, making sure she was fully caught up on all of the requirements of working there.

Deep down, Margot knew that what had happened to her body was a miracle. She knew it had to have something to do with the belly-button piercing, but given how happy she was every time she looked at her reflection, she had a hard time caring. Whatever it was, Margot was not only happy with the results, but she was excited to see what else was in store for her as she started working at the salon.

The hardest part about getting herself to the salon that morning was figuring out what she was going to wear. Her normal clothing simply did not fit her properly anymore. Everything was too big for her now slender frame. It was not just that her clothes looked like large tents, draping over her body, but none of her pants fit. Her underwear didn't even fit.

It took time, but Margot eventually found something she felt was passable. It was an old sundress that had not fit her in years. She had no idea why she had held onto it, but she was now glad she had. The dress was still too big for Margot, but it was passable. That was all she needed until her new coworkers provided her with clothes that better fit her body. Not that she had any idea what kinds of clothes Jaci, Kaci, and Laci would lend her, but considering how they had all been dressed yesterday, she should have asked the question.

When Margot arrived at the salon, the place was already

humming with activity. Jaci and Kaci were both working with women's hair. Laci was in the middle of drawing a tattoo on a woman's wrist. Margot sat down in the waiting area, just as she had the day before, and perused the magazines.

It was only once Jaci was done with her customer that she acknowledged Margot. Not that Margot was upset. It was clear that Jaci had been focused on her customer. Such dedication was impressive. Admittedly, none of the women seemed to be the sorts of people who could multitask. But it was hard to fault them for that when they clearly took their jobs seriously and did such good jobs. Laci's tattoo art looked fantastic.

"Hey girl," Jaci said. "We've got some clothing for you in the back room. Let me show you."

Margot followed close behind, both excited to change into clothing that was likely to fit her, but also to see what kinds of styles had been picked out for her. Considering all three women were wearing cropped tops that showed off their tits and short skirts, she had to imagine that they would choose something similar for her. Margot had a similar waist size to them, although she had no way of matching them in the chest. Maybe someday she would want to get implants or lip filler like the others, but she could only guess how much that would cost her and there was no way she could afford that right now, assuming she wanted fake tits and cocksucking lips.

"These were clothes we bought before we got our tits, so they should fit you pretty good," Jaci explained as she opened a pink suitcase filled to the brim with clothing.

"Thanks so much for this," Margot said, almost wanting to apologize for being such a burden. However, the smile on Jaci's face told her that Jaci was happy to help. It had been her idea, after all.

"You're one of us now," Jaci said. "Take your time changing into something you'd like. Come on out and we'll start getting you ready to do this job for real."

Once Margot was alone, she started sorting through the suitcase, trying to decide what she was going to wear. It was not an easy choice, but everything she saw, even the really skimpy items, seemed more appealing than her shapeless sundress. Not that the dress was shapeless, but it looked that way on her now trim body. What few curves she had left were completely hidden by the ill-fitting dress.

However, it quickly became clear that Margot's guess at the type of clothing she would be provided with was on the money. Not a single top was long enough to cover her midriff. And most of the shorts and skirts would leave almost all of her legs on display, because they were so short. There were no pants, but it was warm enough not to worry about pants, even in the climate controlled salon.

When Margot finally stepped out of the backroom, she had ditched her sundress and instead chosen a white halter top and a pink micro skirt. The two items had no hope in ever touching, but after spending a few minutes in front of a mirror, Margot decided she liked the bare midriff look. And the pink barbell in her belly-button went well with the skirt.

But the deciding factor on this outfit had actually been the high-heeled platform sandals Margot had found sitting next to the suitcase. She had not seen them at first and had been trying to figure out what matched her now oversized sneakers. The problem was that her feet had narrowed. The old her wore wide shoes. The new her could wear normal sized shoes.

Not that there was anything normal about the sandals Margot now wore. She found herself unsteady as she stepped out of the backroom, her balance not used to the high heels or the fact there were at least two inches of sole beneath her toes. But she had to admit they looked good on her. They really helped to emphasize her legs and ass, which Margot now found to be at least somewhat desirable. She might not be able to keep up with the others in the tits department, but her ass was about equal to theirs and they were all wearing heels. Margot needed to keep up.

"There she is," exclaimed one of the women. Margot was not sure which woman was which. They all looked interchangeable. It was surprising to find out that there was no relation between them.

Before Margot knew what was happening, she had been mobbed by all three women. Their total embrace was oddly welcome. Their warmth and excitement to have her there and looking as she now did left Margot almost in tears. These women barely knew her and they were treating her like their best friend. It was wonderful, especially after all the struggles Margot had gone through recently.

It was an interesting experience to have three sets of fake tits pushed into her as she was surrounded by her new coworkers. There was a warming tingle that shot down Margot's spine and went straight to her pussy. It was a reminder that she was not wearing panties. None had been provided for her and none of her own had fit her. She just needed to remember to keep her knees together whenever she sat down.

And she mostly succeeded in that. Margot hung out at the salon all day, observing the work and getting to know her coworkers. By the end of the day, she was pretty sure she could tell the three women apart, but it was difficult. Their voices were a little different and their faces, while remarkably similar, were just different enough where she could start to tell them apart. However, there was no way that Margot could actually describe those differences. It came down to a gut feeling.

Spending the day with Jaci, Kaci, and Laci, Margot quickly figured out that their bimbo acts were no acts. They were dumb and ditzy in almost every way. The only exceptions came in their work. They were expert hair stylists, tattoo artists and body piercers. They could do it all, making them even more interchangeable. Margot figured out that Jaci came first. Then

Kaci joined the team. Laci was the last to become one of the salon bimbos, but the way they were all friends made Margot hopeful that they would accept her, even if she was no bimbo.

However, throughout the day, Margot found herself adopting their speaking habits more and more. By the time the day was over, she was adding superfluous likes to her sentences without even thinking about it.

"You three are, like, the best," Margot said as Jaci locked the front door and turned off the open sign. The salon was mostly by appointment only, so the chances of walk-ins were slim, but they still came in occasionally.

"Come on," Kaci beckoned as she started to sashay toward the backroom. "We've got some drinks. After a day like today, we need to party."

Margot was usually not a big drinker, but she desperately wanted to fit in. She had never been welcomed by coworkers in such a way before and she did not want this to end. If this one day lasted forever, she would be perfectly content.

And before they knew it, they were all tipsy and giggling, especially Margot. It turned out that she got very giggly when she drank, but that only helped her fit in with the others better. It seemed it was only the size of their chests and lips that separated them when they had all been drinking.

"We were supposed to just pierce your tongue tonight," Jaci slurred. "But what if we did her nipples too." As she spoke, she shifted from talking to Margot to talking to Kaci and Laci.

"Yeah, let's do it," the other two said together.

"Wait, what?" Margot asked. She was only half following the situation now. It had been one thing to pierce her belly-button and she was definitely thankful for it, but they wanted to pierce more of her?

"You want to be one of us, don't you?" Jaci asked.

"Of course," Margot answered, but the words flowed out

before she really had a chance to think of what she wanted to say.

"We usually do them one at a time, your tongue and then your nipples, but it would be faster to do them all at once," Kaci explained.

Margot knew that all three women had their tongues and nipples pierced. She was reminded of that every time that they opened their mouths or by simply looking at their chests. They all wore tight enough tops where it was obvious their nipples had been pierced.

"Do you have any other piercings I should be aware of?" Margot asked. Her inebriation seemed to fade in response to this sudden topic of conversation. She was not against any of those piercings, but it still seemed like a lot.

All three women looked at each other and smiled. Then they nodded, looking back at Margot. However, they remained silent as to what those piercings were.

"Let's get her ready, girls," Jaci announced as she set down her drink and stood up. She was joined a moment later by Kaci and Laci. They advanced on Margot, but with smiles on their faces, belying their real intentions.

Margot froze, not sure what was happening, but she somehow knew that even if she did not want to get these piercings, she was going to end up with them anyway. But the fact that, deep down, she did want to be more like her coworkers, she was already agreeing inwardly. She put up no fight when they took her by the arms and led her over to the table. This was where they did the more private tattoos and piercings, away from the eyes out in the main room.

Before Margot knew it, she was lying back and her halter top had been untied, leaving her small breasts bare.

"What first?" Kaci asked. She already had a piercing gun at hand, ready to go.

"Tongue then nipples," Jaci answered. "Keep the order the same, even if there's no real difference."

Margot opened her mouth and Kaci held her tongue tight in a pair of forceps. Then there was the pinching sensation of the piercing gun as it pushed a hole through her tongue. A moment later and a pink stud, just like the ones the other women had, sat in her tongue.

Margot was surprised how little pain there was. She did not even sense that there was that big of a difference in the way her tongue moved in her mouth. There seemed to be little to know swelling. The only difficulty was learning to speak with a stud in her tongue.

The nipples were equally painless. And before she knew it, she had two pink barbells through her nipples. She was done.

By the time Margot left for home that night, she had sobered up. But she smiled at how good she felt. Even if she did not have the big, fake tits of her coworkers, or the plump sexy lips, she now felt more like one of them than she had ever hoped to before. She was certain that when she started work officially, it would be the best job she had ever had.

But first she needed sleep. The moment she walked into her apartment, the pink suitcase in tow, she yawned, craving sleep. She undressed completely, choosing to sleep naked since her pajamas were too big for her, and climbed under the covers. She fell asleep with a smile on her face.

CHAPTER 3

"Holy shit," Margot screamed when she woke up the next morning. As soon as her eyes fluttered open after a night filled with erotic dreams, she sensed that something was different. As she laid on her back, there was an unfamiliar weight on her chest. If Margot had a pet, she would have assumed the animal was perched on her chest, but she had no pet and there was no way that an animal could have gotten into her bedroom during the night.

But everything became clear to her, thus evoking her screaming response, when she looked down and saw the two orbs sticking up off her chest. Her once almost flat chest had been completely altered with large, round tits pushing out from her where her once small breasts had been.

Margot sat up, somehow expecting her tits to move, giving some hint that they followed the laws of physics. However, they remained bolted onto her chest, not sagging in the slightest in response to the pull of gravity.

Wanting to get a better look at herself, Margot quickly threw off the covers and hurried toward her bathroom. The mirror there would tell her what she was dealing with. But the moment she caught sight of her reflection, Margot knew it was not just that she now had fake tits. It was how closely she now looked like her new coworkers. The women she saw in the mirror looked almost identical to Jaci, Kaci, and Laci.

The obvious similarity came in the form of her tits. They were big and round, just like theirs. She shimmied her shoulders back and forth, just to see how they moved. They jiggled and shook, but not in the way a natural pair of tits would. There was a stiffness to them that both made them look incredibly hot on her now thin frame, but also a pliability that just begged to have a pair of hands play with them.

However, even after accounting for her new tits, it was Margot's face that emphasized how similar she now looked to the other stylists. Her lips had plumped up to the point where they almost formed an O-shape when she relaxed her face. And somehow her eyes appeared bigger and her nose smaller, giving her a doll-like complexion that she had only seen among her coworkers and the occasional magazine with heavily airbrushed models.

If any of this bothered Margot, she did not show it. If anything, standing there in her bathroom, seeing her altered body with the cute pink jewelry piercing her nipples and belly-button, and her tongue when she opened her mouth, she had to admit she looked hot. She was turning herself on just by looking at her reflection, her pussy growing wet at the sight of herself.

There was no doubt that Margot looked like a bimbo. She now had a body that appeared designed to turn men on. Some women too. And it was that same body that left her growing more and more aroused by the moment.

"Fuck, you're hot," Margot told her reflection as she reached up and cupped her tits with her hands. After a moment of lifting them and enjoying their enhanced shape, she let her right hand drift down across her midriff to the junction between her legs. She felt so naughty as she started to rub her clit with a finger.

That only served to further amp up her arousal, but it felt so good, so right.

Deep down, Margot knew that she was not supposed to be like this, but it was so hard to argue with the results when she looked this good. She now had a dream body that was almost interchangeable with her colleagues. There was only one difference. While Jaci, Kaci, and Laci looked like bimbos, they were also not that smart. She could see it in their eyes. There was a lack of intelligence in them, something that Margot still had. She might look like a bimbo, but inside, she was still herself.

It did not take long before Margot was ready to leave her apartment. She showered and applied makeup, but her new look did not require much to stand out. Her body spoke for itself already.

There had been some worry about her borrowed clothing fitting her when she opened up the pink suitcase from the day before. She was certain the skirts would still fit her, since her ass and hips had not changed, but she was worried about the tops. Could they stretch over her new tits?

As it turned out, they could, either by almost obscenely stretching over her expanded assets, or by simply tying a halter top differently behind her neck. But no matter what she tried, there was no way to hide the fact that her nipples were pierced. Not that she wanted to. She had quickly grown to like the way her pierced nipples looked in the tight tops she had available to her. It made her feel even sexier.

By the time she was satisfied with her new appearance, Margot walked out of her apartment, not entirely sure where she was going to go. She knew she would end up at the salon eventually, but something told her there was something else for her to do first. Margot was halfway down the stairs to the exit of the building when she practically ran right into one of her neighbors.

"Whoa there," the man said after she bounced off his broad

and muscular chest. Still not fully used to the high heels she wore or her new proportions, Margot found herself starting to fall. It was only through her neighbor's fast actions and strong arms that he caught her, preventing her from tumbling to the ground.

"Oh my," Margot said as she finally found her balance while still being held in her neighbor's arms. She looked up at him, her eyes fluttering. Her core had turned molten as her arousal hit previously unknown heights. "Thank you for catching me."

The man smiled, looking down past her eyes and into her cavernous cleavage. That only turned her libido up higher. To be seen as not only a hot woman, but a sex object, made Margot feel good in a way she had never imagined before. She felt powerful being able to draw such attention. It was a no situation for her, but one she found she liked immensely.

"Hey, why don't we get to know each other better?" the man proposed. "My name is Alex."

It was not a great attempt at a pickup line, but Margot did not care. She wanted to get to know Alex better. She wanted to have a private moment, or many moments, with this hunk of a man.

Margot brought her hand down toward Alex's crotch. She placed her hand on his package, hidden beneath the confines of his pants. She wanted to make her intentions clear. But more than that, before she could respond verbally to his offer, she had a fun thought. Her coworkers all had sexy bimbo names that rhymed. Maybe she could have the same. Her name was Margot, but what if she went by Maci instead?

"I'm Maci," she finally said, deciding to try the name on for size. She might look like a bimbo now, but she still did not think like one. However, there was no good reason why she should not try her hand at acting like one, just for the fun of it. And that was the reason she decided to give herself a bimbo name, inspired by her bimbo colleagues.

After that, however, Margot was not entirely sure how she had ended up in Alex's apartment. The whole thing got a little hazy. Not that she was complaining about the outcome. Kneeling on his bed with him standing in front of her with his muscular chest now bare was not unwelcome. And it was even more fun to reach up behind her neck and untie her halter top, revealing her tits to someone else for the first time.

The moment that Alex's cock sprung into view, Margot's mouth watered, something that had never happened before when she saw a man's cock. She had never known such a thing was actually possible, to salivate at the thought of taking a cock into her mouth. But with her tongue piercing and her plump lips, her mouth was now made to be a receptacle for cocks. And she wanted to test that out for the first time.

Margot practically moaned as she took Alex's cock between her lips for the first time. She had no idea that cocksucking could feel so good to her. She swirled her tongue over and around his cock as she hollowed her cheeks to provide even more pleasure. It was not until she opened her throat to him that she even realized that this was her first blowjob. She had never given one before, not wanting a man's cock to be anywhere near her mouth. But now it was different. She was different.

"Fuck, you've got a perfect mouth for this, Maci." It was a simple statement, but Margot knew it was true. She did not understand how her body had been changed by the piercings she had been given, but she was not about to ignore such a gift, especially when her actions felt so right.

Somehow Margot knew Alex was getting close to cumming. She could sense it. He had not reached his point of no return yet, but she knew that was only a matter of time. But she did not want him to cum in her mouth. Yes, she somehow knew she would enjoy swallowing his seed, but she wanted to fuck her for real, not just her mouth, and she did not want to wait for him to recover.

Margot pulled off of his cock and looked up at him, her still hunched over and looking every bit the submissive bimbo that she projected. "Please, fuck me in my pussy."

For the briefest of moments, Margot thought Alex would refuse. She thought he would grab her by her hair and force his cock back into her mouth. That only served to turn her on more, but she really wanted him to fuck her pussy, even if she was willing to continue sucking his cock if he demanded it of her.

But the look in Alex's eyes told her all she needed to know. He might have liked the blowjob, but he too wanted to fuck her pussy. His eyes grew wild as he pushed Margot back, her body falling backwards onto the bed. He then climbed up as she spread her legs, her skirt riding up. And without wearing panties, there was no thing to get in the way of his cock as he positioned himself between her legs.

"Fuck you're big," Margot moaned as Alex thrust into her for the first time. She had not even noticed how big his cock was, having had so few encounters with men before. But he was big, matching his large body size. Her pussy stretched around his cock as he started with a steady rhythm, letting her velvety folds envelope him with each thrust.

The pleasure was exquisite. Her past sexual experiences were at best cheap imitations of this moment. Her body, completely redesigned for sex, provided her with more pleasure than she could imagine. It only took a few thrusts by Alex before she was a moaning mess, her body barely able to function under the onslaught of pleasure. Her eyes lost their focus as she let herself become a rag sex doll, completely malleable to Alex's movements and desires.

And when he finally came, his hot white cum filling her pussy, she came too, her body convulsing as a cascade of orgasmic pleasure flowed through her in wave after wave. Her vision turned white as it became too much, her mind almost crumbling under the weight of it all.

When Margot finally recovered, she still felt a happy high remaining from her orgasm. Her body tingled in the most delicious way possible, her arousal still at an elevated state. She had no idea that this was likely to be a new normal, where at the very least she was always going to be a little horny. But she was still adapting to life with her new body and it would only be time before she understood the ins and outs of her new life with a bimbo body.

Margot kissed Alex goodbye once she was completely ready to head out again. She could still feel her wetness along her pussy lips, but she had come to terms with that. It would be even more noticeable if she had worn panties with her short skirt. The cool air would have chilled her far more.

However, before Margot left for the salon, now feeling ready to greet her coworkers and to show off all the changes she had undergone overnight, she went back up stairs to her apartment to freshen up her face and to load her cosmetics into a handbag so that she could fix her face the next time an encounter like the one she just had with Alex occurred.

"Hey, girl," Laci exclaimed when Margot stepped into the salon. "I love the tits. They look so good on you like that."

Margot smiled, enjoying the compliment. She found herself among friends. They were more than work colleagues. They really were friends.

The salon had a quiet moment, so Jaci, Kaci, and Laci all came over to hug Margot. The four sexy bimbos embraced each other. Margot had yet to work an official day in her new job, but she knew that would happen soon enough.

"It's time for your last piercing," Jaci announced when the four finally broke the embrace.

Margot was saddened for a moment, having liked the way

her friends felt pressing their bodies against her. They were all so sexy and they made her feel good. But then Jaci's comment struck her. There was another piercing they had in mind for her? On the one hand, she had never been someone interested in such body modifications, but on the other hand, she was happy with everything that had happened to her so far. She loved the way she looked and the way her body felt. The pull to put her new body through its paces was strong, but she saw no reason to not indulge herself.

Kaci and Laci started giggling, their big smiles giving away their excitement at what would prove to be Margot's last step.

"What piercing?" Margot asked, both wary and excited. It was hard not to share in her friends' excitement.

"But first we need to give you a better name," Jaci said. "Something, you know, more fitting and stuff."

"Like Maci?" Margot offered.

There was a moment of stunned silence. It seemed none of the salon bimbos had figured out that Margot was at least partly in on their plan.

"Yes, like Maci," Jaci finally answered. "Johnny will handle the details."

Before the details could be explained to her, the newly named Maci found herself being ushered into the backroom, just as she had before she received her tongue and nipple piercings. This time she did not need to be told to get up on the table. She did so on her own, even though she had no idea what to expect.

"What's gonna happen?" Maci asked once she was settled. She held her knees together to help make sure her skirt did not ride up too much and expose her, even if she knew her friends would all probably see her pussy eventually. Wearing skirts as short as they did, they must have flashed each other regularly without even meaning to.

"We want to pierce your clit," Kaci offered. "It'll look so

pretty. Just like ours." At that, Kaci lifted her skirt to show off her own piercing.

Maci never would have guessed that her friends had such piercings, but she realized she would have found out soon enough. But she had no idea why they wanted to pierce her clit. She knew about clit hood piercings, but she had never actually seen or heard about an actual clit piercing.

"This is, like, the final step," Jaci explained. "Once we pierce your clit, you'll be one of us, completely."

Even if Maci was nervous about what this final piercing could mean, she still nodded her head, giving permission for them to go ahead. Maci spread her legs and let her skirt naturally ride up around her hips, exposing herself to her friends for the first time. But even though they were the type to giggle at almost anything, they did not giggle now. Their faces were serious and focused. This was not a game to them. This was vitally important.

Maci bit her plump lower lip as Jaci and Kaci worked between her legs. She watched them over the crests of her tits, her own body partially blocking her view. It was amazing what had happened to her so far, but she remained in the dark about what this final piercing would do. Would it make her want sex all the time? She already thought that was true. Even now, she could feel her wetness. She was horny. She was always horny now, somewhere on the scale.

Maci let out a little cry as the piercing gun did its work. And then a moment later the new jewelry slipped through the new hole. And as it did, Maci felt a sereneness wash over her that she had never imagined was possible before. Every worry that had flitted through her brain simply disappeared. Her thoughts simplified to the most basic possible. Her knowledge when it came to her work remained, but her cares and worries about everything else seemed to disappear.

As a content smile came to Maci's lips, her eyes began to

dull, the intelligence that she had once had now gone. Maci was a bimbo. And she was a happy and horny bimbo. This was her life now and she loved it.

And just as Maci sat up to look at her new piercing, not even realizing that this one did not require her to sleep for it to take effect, the door to the backroom opened and a man walked in. As soon as Maci looked up, she knew who she was looking at. It was Johnny. He had come to fuck his latest salon bimbo. Maci could not wait. She had never been happier. Margot might not have understood what kind of path she had started on when she first entered the salon, but now her life made sense. She was a bimbo and she worked at the bimbo salon. Nothing could be better, especially when she knew she was about to get fucked.

ABOUT THE AUTHOR

Sadie Thatcher is a longtime author of erotic fiction, especially related to transformations and bimbofication. She likes to say "I have thrown off the shackles of my conservative upbringing and now write erotic stories."

She maintains a special blog devoted to her writings, including a behind the scenes look at her writing process, and bimbos in general, as well as highlights works by other authors. They can be found at:

https://authorsadiethatcher.tumblr.com

twitter.com/Sadie_Thatcher

The Bimbo Professor: The Curse of Playing Bimbo Tag Book 3

Anything for the Job

Anything for the Job 2

Anything for His Job

The Bimbo in the Mirror

The Bimbo in the Mirror 2

Astrid and the Bimbo Bee

Bella and the Bimbo Bee

Cali and the Bimbo Bee

Desiree and the Bimbo Bee

Ember and the Bimbo Bee

Fiona and the Bimbo Bee

The Intern

The Lawyer

The Hacker

Cause & Effect

Witless Protection

Stealing Sally

Trial and Error

Beta Testing

Exposed

Bimbo for a Weekend

Bimbo for a Week

Bimbo for Life

Fake It Until You Make It Season 1

Simple and Fun Volume 1

Simple and Fun Volume 2

Simple and Fun Volume 3

Simple and Fun Volume 4

Simple and Fun Volume 5

Simple and Fun Volume 6

Bimbo Halloween

Bimbo Christmas

Bimbo Technology

Dorm Room Bimbo

Carissa's Magic Pen

Spirit Walk

Muscle Memory

The Case of the Bimbo Wife

Changes

Changes 2

New Year New You

The Bimbo Dream

The Wedding Gift

The Cure

Backfire

Bim & Bo Yoga

Wishing for Each Other

Bimbo Roots

A Bimbo at Oktoberfest

The Lost Bet

The Fountain

Bimbo Ghost

Sugar and Spice and Everything Nice

Basic Bimbo

A Helping Hand

Bimbos in Space

Christmas Train to Bimboton

Letters to Bimbo Claus

Gone Fishing

The Bimbo Behind the Mask

Rival Wishes

What's in a Name?

Playing the Game

Friendly Wishes

My Chemical Bimbo

To Be Young Again

Something Bimbo Calls Him Home

Wishing for Him

The Author Gets Bimbofied

Bigfoot and the Bimbo

Bimbo Zero

Going Native

Thanks for Giving

Working for Bimbo Claus

The Spirit of Bimbo Christmas

The Bimbo Sweater

What Really Happened to D.B. Cooper

Starting Over

Milk and Bliss

The Fighter

The Help

Body Swap Rings: Happy Anniversary

Body Swap Rings 2: Wedding Night

The Bimbo Experience

The Bimbo Experience 2

The Bimbo Experience 3some

The 4th Bimbo Experience

Bimbo Genes

Bimbo Genes II: The Virus

The Bimbo Genes III: The Epidemic

Bimbo Juice: Blue Raspberry

Bimbo Juice: Grape

Bimbo Juice: Mango

Bimbo Juice: Pineapple

Bimbo Juice: Red Apple

Bimbo Juice: Veggie

Bimbo Juice Gone Wild: The Muse

Bimbo Juice Gone Wild: Street Racer

Bimbo Juice Gone Wild: Score

Bimbos of the Traveling Earrings: Book 1

Bimbos of the Traveling Earrings: Book 2

Bimbos of the Traveling Earrings: Book 3

Bimbos of the Traveling Earrings: Book 4

Bimbo Party: Kennedy

Bimbo Party: Esme

Bimbo Party: Ariana

Bimbo Party: Tara

Workout Buddies

Wishful Thinking

Wanting More

Bimbo Harem: Annabelle

Bimbo Harem: Josie

Bimbo Harem: Nikki

Bimbo Harem: Tiana

Giggle Dust

Giggle Dust 2.0

Giggle Dust 3.0

Giggle Dust 4.0

Bimbo Takeover: The First Step

Bimbo Takeover: Teammates

Bimbo Takeover: Going to the Top

Bimbo Takeover: Revenge of the Bimbos

Thanks for the Mammaries

A New Beginning

Copying Kat

Spreading the Love

Discovering Eden

Building Eden

Spring In Eden

Saving Eden

The Perfect Girlfriend

The Perfect Engagement

The Perfect Wife

The Perfect Woman

Be Hot, Not Smart

No Thoughts for Thots

Be Art, Not Smart

The Cream of the Crop

A New Kind of Passion

www.ingramcontent.com/pod-product-compliance
Lightning Source LLC
Chambersburg PA
CBHW031448150726
47990CB00007B/2662